DRAWING AGAINST SIX OF A KIND

Canyon O'Grady didn't mind a gamble—but not against these odds.

He had one gun at his side, and two men on his other side in the crowded saloon. His old friend, ex-sheriff Tom Wilmot, was staring at his cards in a game of poker. The green new sheriff, Dan Fisher, was looking into his beer. Canyon alone saw the gunmen enter the crowded room two by two until there were six of them ready to close in for the kill.

Six against three, and two of the three sitting ducks, Canyon reckoned. The only questions were, when would the shooting start—and who would be alive at the end . . . ?

COLORADO AMBUSH

by

Jon Sharpe

A SIGNET BOOK

SIGNET
Published by the Penguin Group
Penguin Books USA Inc., 375 Hudson Street
New York, New York 10014, U.S.A.
Penguin Books Ltd, 27 Wrights Lane,
London W8 5TZ, England
Penguin Books Australia Ltd, Ringwood,
Victoria, Australia
Penguin Books Canada Ltd, 10 Alcorn Avenue,
Toronto, Ontario, Canada M4V 3B2
Penguin Books (N.Z.) Ltd, 182–190 Wairau Road,
Auckland 10, New Zealand

Penguin Books Ltd, Registered Offices:
Harmondsworth, Middlesex, England

First published by Signet, an imprint of New American Library,
a division of Penguin Books USA Inc.

First Printing, November, 1992
10 9 8 7 6 5 4 3 2

Printed in Canada

Canyon O'Grady

His was a heritage of blackguards and poets, fighters and lovers, men who could draw a pistol and bed a lass with the same ease.

Freedom was a cry seared into Canyon O'Grady, justice a banner of his heart.

With the great wave of those who fled to America, the new land of hope and heartbreak, solace and savagery, he came to ride the untamed wildness of the Old West

With a smile or a six-gun, Canyon O'Grady became a name feared by some and welcomed by others, but remembered by all . . .

Colorado Territory, 1861—
a new territory not immune
to old violences. . . .

1

When Canyon O'Grady first rode into the town of Rayford, Colorado, he had no idea the chain of events his arrival would set off. After completing an assignment in Denver he had simply decided to visit an old friend who lived nearby—well, not far away, actually . . . that is, if you could call a hundred miles not far away. In any case, he and Cormac had covered the distance in two and a half days and were tired when they arrived.

Upon completion of his assignment in Denver Canyon had sent word to his boss in Washington, Major General Rufus Wheeler, that he would be taking a short detour to Rayford. In return he had gotten a typically cryptic reply from Wheeler, who wrote: Short by whose standards? He had not bothered to answer.

Canyon's friend was a man named Tom Wilmot. He lived just outside of Rayford on a small ranch with his wife, Olivia. However he was also the sheriff of Rayford. Consequently, Canyon expected to find him in town in the middle of the day.

Canyon had been to Rayford before, but not for a long time. He tried to think of the last time he had seen Tom and Olivia, and it had to be . . . years. He couldn't think how many. He rode directly to the livery stable and handed Cormac over to the liveryman for care.

"Be stayin' long?" the man asked. He was a grizzled old codger who looked as if he was in his sixties. He had strong hands though. Canyon noticed that. Although thin, there was nothing frail about the man.

"I don't know," Canyon said. "A few days, maybe."

"Well, I'll take good care of 'im," the man said, "don't you worry none."

"I won't," Canyon said. "Thanks."

The redhaired agent collected his saddlebags and rifle and walked over to the hotel with them. When he got there he was pleasantly surprised. Since he had last been there the place had been cleaned up and repairs made. The lobby was actually a pleasant place—made even more so by the fact that behind the desk was a lovely young woman. She had thick, long dark hair that hung to her shoulders, dark eyebrows, and full lips that were almost plum colored. Canyon noticed that she was full breasted, but the desk kept him from noticing anything else. He hoped that from the waist down she was as finely formed.

He approached the desk and she looked up at him with wide, brown, appraising eyes. That was all right with him. He had been doing the same to her only seconds before. What's fair is fair, Canyon always said.

Up close she appeared to be in her late twenties.

"Can I help you?" she asked. Her voice was well modulated, just a step away from being husky. During sex, though, he was sure it would become husky.

"I'd like a room, please."

"Surely," she said. She turned the register around so he could sign it. "How long will you be staying?"

"I'm not sure," he said. "I'm just here to visit a friend."

"Oh? Who would that be?"

"Sheriff Wilmot."

"*Sheriff Wilmot?*" she asked, her voice sounding strange.

"That's right," he said, turning the register back to her.

"I see," she said. She read the book, where he'd signed CANYON O'GRADY, WASHINGTON, D.C. "All the way from Washington?"

"Not really," he said. "I was in Denver when I decided to ride over."

"I see," she said, again.

"Is something wrong?" he asked.

"Uh, no, nothing," she said, shaking her head. She turned to take a key from a slot and he took the opportunity to inspect her from the waist down. She had wide hips and a fine, firm ass. From head to toe, then, she was a lovely woman.

"You'll be in number four, Mr. O'Grady."

"Fine."

"The dining room is open until nine."

"The last time I was here the food in the dining room wasn't that good," he said frankly.

"That must have been some time ago," she said.

"It was."

"Then the food must have been terrible," she said, smiling. "My father and I have changed that since we took over the hotel last year."

"I see," he said. "Well then, I'll have to give it a try."

"I'm sure you'll find the food vastly improved," she said.

"I've already found the hotel much improved," he said, "so I'm confident that you are right."

"See you later, then," she said, "I mean, when you come down for dinner."

"Yes," he said, "later." He started away, toward the steps, then turned back and said, "Excuse me, but what's your name?"

She smiled and said, "Erica—my name is Erica Gardner, Mr. O'Grady."

"It's nice to meet you, Erica," he said.

"And nice to meet you, Mr. O'Grady. I hope you enjoy your stay."

He went up the steps to the second floor, scolding himself. He mustn't let a fine-looking woman make him forget why he had come here in the first place, to see an old friend.

There would be time enough for Erica Gardner later.

Although he was tired O'Grady decided to go and find Wilmot right away and buy him a drink. He exchanged smiles with Erica Gardner on his way out and walked to the sheriff's office. He knocked on the door and tried the door knob. The door was locked. He knocked again and when there was no answer, he decided to go and have a drink himself and then try again later.

Canyon entered the first saloon he came to. When he was last in Rayford it had been called the Golden Shoe Saloon. Now there was a sign hanging over the entrance that said it was BOONE'S SALOON. When he entered, it still looked like the Golden Shoe.

He walked to the bar and ordered a beer. The bartender was a man in his late thirties, with an unruly shock of black hair and what looked like a two-day growth of beard. He had a habit of rubbing his hand over the stubble. It made a very audible scratching sound.

"You look worn out," the bartender said, setting a mug of beer down in front of him.

"I am," Canyon said, picking up the beer. "I just rode in from Denver. Two and a half days."

"Two and a half days from Denver?" the bartender said. "You must have a good horse."

"I do."

"And you must have really pushed him."

"I'm afraid I did," Canyon said. He finished the beer and set the empty mug down.

"Another?"

"Why not?" Canyon said. "I've got some time to kill."

The bartender drew a second beer and asked, "Got an appointment?"

"Not an appointment," the agent said. "I just have to stop in and see a friend."

"You got a friend here in town?" the man asked.

"That's right," Canyon said. He took a sip of beer, intending for this one to last longer.

"What's his name?" the man asked. "Maybe I know him . . . or is it a her?"

"No," O'Grady said, "it's a man. In fact, it's the sheriff."

"Oh yeah?" the bartender said. "You know Dan Fisher?"

"Dan Fisher?" Canyon said, not recognizing the name.

"Well . . . yeah," the bartender said, frowning, "that's who the sheriff is."

"But that's not right," O'Grady said, puzzled. "The sheriff of Rayford is Tom Wilmot."

"Wilmot?" the bartender said. "He *was* the sheriff."

O'Grady put the beer down and asked, "What do you mean, he *was* the sheriff?"

"I mean he ain't the sheriff no more."

"Since when?"

"Jesus . . . it must be six, maybe eight months now," the man said with a shrug.

"What happened?"

The man opened his mouth to answer, then stopped and thought a moment.

"Mister, are you really friends with Tom Wilmot?" he finally asked.

"Yes, I am," Canyon said. "Why?"

"Maybe I shouldn't say any more," the bartender said. "Maybe you should talk to Mrs. Wilmot."

"Mrs. . . . is Tom dead, then?"

"No," the bartender said, "no, he ain't dead . . . but he don't talk much, anymore."

"Look—"

"Mister," the man said, holding up one hand, "please, maybe you should talk to the lady. You know her, don't you?"

"Of course I know Mrs. Wilmot," Canyon said. "Tom *and* Olivia are my friends."

"Go and see them, then," the bartender said. "They'll tell you what happened."

"Do they still live on their ranch?"

"They sure do."

"Then I'll go out there. What do I owe you for the beers?"

"That's okay," the man said. "I'm Boone. This is my place. The beers are on the house."

"Thanks, Boone," Canyon said and left the saloon in a hurry. On the way out he remembered the odd look Erica Gardner had given him earlier when he mentioned Sheriff Wilmot.

The Tom Wilmot that Canyon O'Grady knew would never have given up his badge willingly. If he wasn't sheriff of Rayford anymore, there must be a damned good reason—or a damned *bad* one!

Just how good or bad it was he was obviously going to have to find out from Tom Wilmot himself.

2

Canyon saddled Cormac himself and was riding out of the livery when a man appeared in front of him. The man was wearing a badge.

"In a hurry?" the man asked.

"As a matter of fact, yes," Canyon said, "I am."

"Maybe you'll take a few minutes to talk to me?"

"Are you Sheriff Fisher?"

"That's right."

"I guess I don't have much choice then, do I?"

"Not much," the lawman said. "Why don't you just ride over to my office. It won't take very long."

With that the man turned and walked away at a brisk pace. Canyon watched him go, giving him a good head start, and then rode Cormac over to the man's office. As he dismounted the sheriff unlocked the door and entered. When O'Grady walked in the lawman was already seated behind his desk. He appeared to be in his late twenties, although with his hat off his brown hair was already rather sparse.

"You just got into town today, didn't you?" the man asked.

"That's right."

"And your name?"

"Don't you know all of this already?" O'Grady asked.

"Humor me."

The man sounded fairly well educated.

"My name is Canyon O'Grady."

"From where?"

"Lots of places."

"The hotel register said Washington, D.C."

"You have to write something in a hotel register, don't you?"

After a moment the man said, "I suppose you do. How long are you intending to stay in town, Mr. O'Grady?"

"That depends."

"On what?"

"I don't know," Canyon said. "On the town, I guess."

"Are you here to see anyone in particular, Mr. O'Grady," Fisher asked, "or are you just passing through?"

"I stopped into town to see some friends," O'Grady admitted.

"And who might those friends be?"

"Maybe you know them," Canyon said. "Tom and Olivia Wilmot?"

"Of course I know the Wilmots," the sheriff said. "Have you known them long?"

"Yes." Canyon had decided not to offer anything beyond the answers to direct questions.

"But you haven't seen them in some time?"

"No."

"Then you don't know about the bad luck that's befallen them?"

"No, I don't," Canyon said, and it was all the red-haired agent could do *not* to ask the lawman what he was talking about.

"Well," the man said, leaning forward in his seat,

"take my word for it, they've fallen on some bad times. I'm thinking maybe they wouldn't want you to see them the way they are right now."

"I might be able to help."

"I doubt it."

Canyon leaned forward in his seat and said, "If you don't mind I'd rather let them be the judge of that—that is, unless you're warning me off?"

"I'm not warning anyone, Mr. O'Grady," Fisher said, sitting back in his chair now, "I'm just giving out some friendly advice."

"Well, I'll tell you what, Sheriff," Canyon said, "I'll keep your advice in mind. Now, if there's nothing else, I *was* on my way somewhere in a hurry."

"Well," Fisher said with a humorless smile, "I won't detain you any longer."

"Thanks."

Outside the agent paused, wondering just what the hell that was all about. It didn't seem to him like a normal case of a lawman questioning a stranger in town. There seemed to be something else behind, or underlying, the sheriff's questions.

He decided to think about it later. Right now he had other, more important, things on his mind. He mounted up and headed out of town in the direction of the Wilmot ranch.

When Canyon reached the ranch he was surprised at the run-down condition of it. It had never been a big spread, but it had always been well cared for. Now the house, the barn, and the corral were all in a state of disrepair. Once again O'Grady realized that the Tom Wilmot who lived here now couldn't be the same man he knew. Wilmot had been almost obsessive about keeping the ranch up. The town fathers had wanted him to live in town, but he had argued that he would take the job only if he could continue to live on his ranch. The town council had wanted him so badly that they had agreed.

Canyon dismounted and tied Cormac off to a hitching post that was still standing. He stepped up onto the porch, knocked on the door, and took a step back. He wasn't quite sure what to expect. When it opened and he saw Olivia Wilmot standing there he was relieved—but only for a moment. Almost immediately he saw how she had changed. Olivia had always been a beautiful woman, and she still was, but he saw how she had lost weight. She was much too thin, so much so that her cheekbones looked as if they might cut through her cheeks.

"O'Grady?" she said, frowning. She stepped outside and said, "Canyon O'Grady?"

"Hello, Olivia."

"My God . . ." she said, and rushed into his arms. He was surprised but managed to catch her. She slumped against him and might have fallen if he hadn't supported her.

"Olivia, what's wrong?" he asked.

"Oh, Canyon," she said into his chest, "I don't know where to start."

"Start with Tom, Olivia," he said. "Where is he? What happened to him?"

She looked up at him and said, "Come inside, Canyon, and I'll tell you everything."

The inside of the house was in considerably better order than the outside, but then that had always been Olivia's domain.

"What happened, Olivia?" he asked. "What's going on? I came to town to see some old friends, and everyone started acting strange when I asked for Sheriff Tom Wilmot."

"Tom's not sheriff anymore, Canyon," she said, sadly.

"I know that much," he said. "In fact, that's all I know. I need to know why. What happened?"

She moved to the kitchen table and sat down heavily, her eyes cast downward.

"There was a shooting seven months ago, Canyon," she said after a few moments. "A bad one. For a while . . . for a while we didn't know if Tom would live."

"But he did."

"Yes."

"And he recovered?"

She didn't answer.

"When he finally got back on his feet," she said instead, "he wanted to continue his job . . . but by that time the town council had replaced him."

"With this fella Dan Fisher?"

"That's right," she said. "Fisher was Tom's first deputy. He managed to convince the town fathers that even after Tom had recovered, he'd make a better sheriff."

"And they believed him?"

"Yes," she said. She looked at him and her eyes were wet. "Just when he needed that badge the most, Canyon, they took it away from him. They didn't even offer him a job as a deputy."

"He was the sheriff here for what, eight years?" Canyon asked.

"Nine."

He shook his head and said, "There's no loyalty."

She didn't reply.

"Everything went bad after that. He wasn't working

as a lawman, and he *couldn't* work around the ranch. The place got run down . . . and so did I."

"Olivia," Canyon said, "you are as beautiful as ever."

"And you're as much of a liar as you ever were," she said with a wan smile.

"But why won't he work around the ranch?" Canyon asked. "As I remember this place could have supported you both if Tom *wasn't* working as the sheriff."

"It's not that he won't work," she said, "it's that he can't."

"Was the injury that bad?"

"It was horrible," she said, closing her eyes.

"Olivia," he said, moving to her side and crouching down next to her, "why not move on, make a life somewhere else?"

She looked at him and said, "Because I can't convince him that there *is* still a life to be made, somewhere."

He put his hand over hers and said, "Maybe I can help. Maybe I can talk to him."

"You can talk to him," she said, "but I don't think it will do any good."

"Why don't we wait and see? When will he be back?"

"He should be back anytime, now." She stood up and said, "I'll make some coffee. Would you like some coffee?"

"Sure," he said, because it would give her something to do.

As she moved to the stove he said, "Olivia, what happened to the men who shot Tom?"

"They were never caught."

"Who were they?"

"Just a gang," she said.

"How many?"

"Five . . . I think there were five."

"Did they hunt for them? The new sheriff, I mean? Did he put together a posse?"

"Not really," she said. "There was no new sheriff for a while, and then too much time had gone by."

"What about Tom?" O'Grady asked. "Didn't he want to go after them after he got on his feet?"

"I wish he did want to go after them," she said. "It would give his life some purpose."

"I don't understand," he said. "Tom was never the kind of man to let something like this go unpunished. I mean, if it's as bad as you indicate, why wouldn't he hunt for them? Even after all this time?"

She stopped doing what she was doing and said with her back still to him, "There's something I haven't told you, Canyon."

"What's that?"

"About . . . the injury . . ." she said, haltingly, "it was—" but she was interrupted by the front door opening.

Canyon turned to face the door and watched his friend Tom Wilmot enter. He opened his mouth to greet him but stopped when Wilmot had completely entered the room and closed the door. He wanted to speak but couldn't. He couldn't even look at his friend's face because his eyes were drawn to the empty right sleeve of Tom Wilmot's shirt—where his right arm used to be.

3

Later O'Grady and Wilmot were sitting outside on the porch with cups of coffee. From inside came the smells of the dinner Olivia was preparing.

Tom sat in a chair with the cup on the floor on his left side. Canyon sat with the cup in his right hand, feeling guilty about *having* a right hand.

No wonder Wilmot couldn't work around the ranch—and was it no wonder that the town council had replaced him? Could they really have expected to take back a sheriff who had only one arm?

"Sorry for the shock," Tom said, breaking into Canyon's reverie. "Olivia should have told you."

"It's . . . all right," Canyon said, feeling that the comment was inane, but he couldn't think of anything else to say.

He felt bad that when Tom Wilmot had entered the house all he had been able to do was stare at his empty right sleeve. It was probably the reaction Tom had gotten from everyone else; he didn't need to get it from a friend.

"Don't blame yourself," Wilmot said, as if reading his friend's mind. "I stare at it myself, some days. When I woke up and . . . and saw that it was gone, I wanted to die. I started screaming at the doctor, asking him why he didn't just let me die instead of doing . . . doing *this* to me."

"Tom, I—"

"Don't know what to say, right?" Wilmot finished for him. "There *is* nothing to say, Canyon. Nothing to say and nothing to do."

O'Grady had never seen Tom Wilmot so . . . defeated. A tall man who had always had a ramrod straight back, broad shoulders, and narrow hips, Wilmot now sat slumped in his chair, and from shoulders to hips he was almost as narrow from one to the other. Wilmot had changed even more drastically than Olivia had. In appearance he had aged so that he looked almost ten years older than he was. His face was gaunt, his hair unruly and graying. He had all the demeanor of a sick man—and yet, but for the missing arm, he was probably as healthy as Canyon himself. How did you convince someone of that, however? How would Canyon have felt if it was he who had lost his right arm? What good was a sheriff—or a Secret Service agent—with no gun hand?

Canyon was about to say something when Olivia came to the door and announced that dinner was ready.

At dinner Canyon watched Olivia cut Tom's food for him so he could eat with only one hand. The man's movements were awkward, and at one point he knocked over his cup, spilling the contents across the table.

"Damn!" Tom swore. "Sorry," he said to Canyon. "Still can't get used to doing everything left-handed."

Olivia cleaned up the mess without saying anything. Canyon was sure they had been through this scene many times before.

After dinner Olivia cleaned off the table, put out a

pot of coffee and two cups, and then excused herself and went into the house's bedroom.

"It's been hard on her," Tom said. "I wonder why she's stayed with me this long."

"No you don't."

Wilmot looked at O'Grady and said, "Yeah, you're right, I don't. I'm just grateful that she has."

"Then maybe you should show her how grateful you are," Canyon suggested.

"How would you suggest I do that?"

"By getting back on your feet and fixing this place up, for one."

Wilmot gave O'Grady a long look.

"What the hell are you're talkin' about?" he finally said.

"I'm talking about stopping feeling sorry for yourself and starting to live again." Canyon was shocked by his own words. He certainly hadn't planned to talk to his friend in this manner, but before he knew it the words were coming out.

"Do you know what you're sayin'?" Wilmot asked. "Do you know what you're lookin' at?"

"Why don't you tell me what I'm looking at?"

"A cripple," Wilmot said, viciously lashing out at himself with the word. "A goddamned cripple, that's what you're lookin' at!"

This last was said so loudly that Olivia came rushing into the room, just as Wilmot stood up, overturning his chair. She stood when she saw her husband standing and glaring at O'Grady.

"Is this what you want?" Wilmot demanded. "You want to see me on my feet? Well, here I am, a one-armed man standing on his feet—and in case you haven't noticed, it's my *right* arm that's gone!"

"I've noticed, Tom," Canyon said, "but in case *you*

haven't noticed you still have one left. You also have two legs, a ranch, a wife, and a friend who's willing to help you."

Wilmot's mouth turned ugly and said, "What do you know about it? What the *hell* do you know!"

Before O'Grady could reply Wilmot turned and stormed out the door, leaving it hanging open in his wake.

Olivia, who had been standing there with both hands covering her mouth, ran to the door and called out after him, "Tom!"

"Let him go, Olivia," Canyon said.

She turned on him and said, "How could you? You're supposed to be his friend."

"I am his friend," Canyon said. "That's why I want him to stop feeling sorry for himself and start living again, for his sake and yours."

She stood there staring at him, and he moved to her in time to grab her and keep her from falling. She buried her face into his chest and sobbed and sobbed . . .

Olivia had gone to bed long before, and Canyon was sitting on the porch with a bottle of whiskey when Tom Wilmot finally returned. He looked like an apparition coming out of the dark into the light thrown from the open door.

When he reached the house Canyon handed him the bottle of whiskey. Tom took a long pull and handed it back.

"Okay," he said to Canyon, "so you're right. I'm still alive and I should start living again . . . it's just so hard."

"You've got Olivia to help you, Tom," Canyon said, "and me."

"I know."

"Why didn't you write me?" Canyon asked. "In all this time why didn't you let me know what happened?"

"I didn't want you to see me like this," Wilmot said simply. "Pride, I guess, or shame."

"You've got nothing to be ashamed of, Tom."

Wilmot sat down on the steps and accepted the bottle again.

"They picked me apart, Canyon," he said, "they just picked me apart."

O'Grady remained silent while his friend nursed the bottle again. He figured he'd let Wilmot tell the story in his own time.

"They rode into town, five of them, and I *knew* they were trouble. I could *feel* it, you know?"

O'Grady knew. It was an instinct men like he and Wilmot developed over the years.

"If I had braced them early, with my deputies, I might have been able to get them out of town, but I didn't. I decided to leave them be as long as they behaved."

He handed the bottle back to O'Grady, who took a swallow.

"They came for me one night, just knocked on the door to draw me out. I stepped outside like some tinhorn and they picked me apart." He paused for a moment, as if fixing the story in his mind. "I don't even think they wanted to kill me. They put a bullet in my left leg, one in my right thigh, one in my side, one in my hand—my right hand—and then my right arm. The doctor said that none of the wounds was fatal by itself, but combined . . . well, I almost died." Again he paused to look at something only he could see, something inside of himself before continuing. "There was too much damage to my arm and hand, the doc said, and he had to take it in order to save my life."

"And what happened to the gang?" Canyon asked.

Tom hesitated and then said, "They came back the next day and robbed the bank, killing two tellers—a man and a woman—and then killing two bystanders outside when my deputies tried to stop them, as well as one of my deputies, a youngster named Kevin Wills." Wilmot shook his head. "Kevin was twenty. He wanted to be a deputy so bad that I decided to go ahead and swear him in and teach him. I got him killed."

"That's crazy."

"Is it?" Tom asked. "Maybe."

He stood up and looked at Canyon.

"I'm goin' to bed. Make yourself comfortable wherever you can."

As Wilmot moved for the door O'Grady said, "Tom, I plan on staying awhile."

Wilmot stopped at the door, said over his shoulder, "We'll talk in the morning," and went inside.

Canyon nodded as his friend went inside, then examined the remainder of the whiskey in the bottle. He had two choices. He could finish it himself and turn in, or he could turn in right now.

Ah, what the hell. There wasn't that much left anyway, was there?

4

Canyon was already awake and had coffee ready when Olivia Wilmot came out of the bedroom.

"I was coming out to make coffee," she said.

"It's made," he said with a smile. "Have a cup."

She poured herself a cup and tasted it while standing at the stove.

"It's awful," she said.

"I knew it would be," he said, "but it's the thought that counts."

"I know it is," she said. "Thank you."

She walked to the table and sat across from him.

"And thank you for last night."

"What did I do last night?"

"I don't know, exactly," she said, "but it seems to have worked."

"What do you mean?"

She put her cup down on the table and leaned forward. He noticed then that there was a gleam in her eyes that wasn't there the night before. She had just gotten up and her hair was a mess and yet she was *radiant*.

"When Tom came to bed last night he couldn't sleep."

"And that was good?"

"He wanted to *talk*," she said. "Canyon, he hasn't wanted to talk since—well, since he lost his arm."

"What did he talk about?" Canyon asked.

"His *arm*!" she said. "I mean . . . he has *never* talked about it. Last night he talked about how it felt to lose it, what it felt like to be without it . . . Canyon, he just *talked* to me, and it was glorious."

Canyon smiled and said, "I'm glad."

"And then . . ." she said, blushing, ". . . and then we made love. We hadn't done *that* since the injury."

He reached across the table to touch her hand and said again, "I'm glad, Olivia, but maybe it had more to do with you than with me."

"No," she said, shaking her head, "it was you. What you said to him yesterday, and last night, it made him think. I haven't been able to do that in seven months."

She picked up her cup as if she were going to drink from it, then looked at him and asked, "Would you mind if I made another pot?"

He smiled and said, "No, I don't mind. In fact, I'd appreciate it."

She stood up and said, "And I'll make breakfast. Eggs? Potatoes—and bacon?"

He watched as she cooked and noticed a spring in her step that was also not there yesterday. Neither was there the defeated slump to her shoulders. He wasn't sure that he could take complete credit for this. Maybe it was just time for Tom Wilmot to wake up. Still, even if he had a little to do with it, he felt a great satisfaction in helping a friend—*both* of his friends, in fact.

Tom Wilmot came out sometime later, sniffing the air.

"It smells good," he said.

Olivia looked at him and said, "Tom . . . you put your shirt on."

"I thought it was about time I started dressing myself, honey," he said.

The shirt was on, but was not completely buttoned. Wilmot was still working on the buttons with his single hand.

"Still having some trouble with the buttons," he said, "but I'll work that out. Is breakfast ready yet? I'm starved. How about you, Canyon?"

"I'm starved, too," O'Grady said.

"It's ready, and it's coming," she said.

Wilmot sat down and Olivia served them both breakfast, and then made a plate for herself. Tom ate with an appetite Canyon could tell had not been there for a long time. Olivia was obviously delighted to watch her husband eat, and ate very little herself.

After she cleared the table and gave them both another cup of coffee, she excused herself to go and get dressed.

"I guess she must have told you," Wilmot said.

"She told me some, Tom."

"All, is more like it," Wilmot said. "Not that I mind. You saved my life, old friend."

"How did I do that?"

"You talked to me like nobody else has in seven months," Wilmot said, then added, "not that I have many friends around here who might have done it."

"The last time I was here you had a lot of friends, Tom," Canyon said.

"Oh sure," Wilmot said, "but see, they wanted to be friends with Tom Wilmot the sheriff, not Tom Wilmot the crip—the one-armed man. See, they think that this"—he indicated his missing arm, pointing to it with his remaining hand—"makes me half a man."

"They're wrong."

"Damn right they're wrong," Wilmot said, "and I plan to prove it to them. I'll need your help, Canyon, if you've got the time."

"I'll make the time, Tom," Canyon said. "You just tell me what you want me to do."

"As soon as I figure that out," Wilmot said, "you'll be the first to know."

Later Wilmot and O'Grady agreed that the first thing that had to be done was repairs around the place.

"I'll take your buckboard into town and pick up some supplies," Canyon said. "Why don't you stay here and figure out a schedule for us."

"No," Wilmot said. "I think I'll come into town with you. It's been months since I been there."

Canyon looked past his friend to Olivia, who nodded, and he said, "Okay, Tom. Let's go."

On the way to town O'Grady asked Wilmot about Dan Fisher.

"What about him?"

"He braced me yesterday when I was on my way out here," Canyon explained. "He just about warned me off, Tom. What's his problem?"

"I don't know," Wilmot said. "I haven't seen Dan in a long time. He was always real ambitious, Canyon, and when I went down he wasted no time stepping into my boots."

"Trying to step into your boots," Canyon corrected his friend. "I doubt that he can fill them."

"Maybe not," Wilmot said, "but Fisher was always a good man, Canyon. He probably makes a good sheriff, but I don't think I'll ever forgive him for the way he went about getting the job."

"I wouldn't, either," Canyon said. "But it still puzzles me why he'd try to warn me away from seeing you. I *thought* it was out of concern for you and Olivia, but . . ."

"I doubt that," Wilmot said. "Like I said, I ain't seen him in a long time. That don't sound like somebody who was real concerned about me and Olivia."

"Maybe we should stop in and say hello to your old deputy, eh?"

Wilmot thought that over a moment and then said, "Maybe we should . . ."

When they reached town Canyon directed the buckboard to the general store. He dropped to the ground and watched carefully as Wilmot awkwardly did the same. He noticed that other people were watching as well. Together they walked into the store.

As they approached the counter the man behind it looked up and registered surprise on his face, which he quickly followed with a broad smile.

"Tom, is that you?"

"It's me, Abe."

"Well, by God, it's good to see you. I haven't seen you in months."

"Abe, this is a friend of mine, Canyon O'Grady," Wilmot said. "Canyon, Abe Gorman."

"Good to meet you, O'Grady," Gorman said.

"Likewise," Canyon said, but he did not offer his hand.

"Abe is president of our Town Council," Wilmot said.

That meant he was one of the men who gave Dan Fisher the sheriff's job.

"What can I do for you today, Tom? How's Olivia?"

"She's fine, Abe."

"The missus keeps meaning to get out to see her," Gorman said.

"Pretty busy though, huh?" Wilmot asked.

"Yeah, busy," Gorman said. "You know how it is."

"Sure," Wilmot said, "I know how it is, Abe. I'll tell Olivia you were askin' about her."

"Please do," Gorman said, awkwardly. "Uh, now what was it I could do for you?"

"I need some supplies, Abe," Wilmot said.

"Well, sure, Tom, just tell me what you need."

Wilmot hesitated a moment and then asked, "Is my credit still good, Abe?"

Now it was Gorman's turn to hesitate before he finally said, "Hey, you know your credit is always good here, Tom. Just tell me what you need."

"It's all written down there," Wilmot said, handing the man the list Olivia had made out.

Gorman looked the list over and said, "I can fill this for you easy, Tom. Just give me a few minutes."

"My buckboard is outside, Abe," Wilmot said. "We have a few other errands to run."

"I'll take care of this for you, Tom. You can count on me."

"I know I can, Abe," Wilmot said. "I could always count on you, couldn't I?"

He stared boldly at the other man, who almost withered beneath the look.

"Uh, s-sure, Tom," Gorman said haltingly. "You always could."

"Yeah," Wilmot said. "I'll be back soon, Abe."

O'Grady followed Wilmot outside, where the man stopped by his buckboard.

"That sonofabitch!"

"Easy, Tom . . . " Canyon said.

"No, this is good, Canyon," Tom said. "I'm feelin'

anger, and that's good. For a long time all I could feel was . . . pity for myself."

"Well then, by all means, anger is an improvement."

Tom looked at Canyon, smiled and said, "One *helluva* improvement."

Canyon clapped his friend on the back and asked, "Where to next?"

"Let's arrange for the delivery of the lumber we need," Wilmot said, "and then we'll go and pay a surprise visit on my old deputy."

"I'm looking forward to that," Canyon said.

5

They arranged for the lumber with a man named Victor Morris, who Wilmot told O'Grady was also a member of the town council. Once again Wilmot asked about his credit and was assured that it was more than good.

"Tom," Canyon said after they had left Morris, "if you need money—"

"To hell with them, Canyon," Wilmot said. "Let them extend me credit. I haven't asked any of them for anything for months, not since I asked for my job back and was refused."

"All right," Canyon said, "but if you need it, it's there."

"I'll remember. Let's go and see Dan Fisher."

"I'm looking forward to this," O'Grady said.

They walked over to the sheriff's office and entered without knocking. Dan Fisher was seated behind his desk and looked up in surprise as they entered. He was even more surprised when he saw who it was.

"Tom . . . " Fisher said, getting to his feet. "What are you doing here?"

"Surprised to see me, Dan?"

"Well . . . no, Tom, not surprised, I'm pleased to see you. I, uh, I've been meaning to get out to the ranch to see you, but . . . "

"I know, Dan," Wilmot said, "you've been busy."

"Well, yeah . . . I mean, you know how it is, you were sheriff for a long time."

"Yes, I was, Dan," Wilmot said, "for a very long time."

There was an awkward silence as Dan Fisher began shifting from one foot to the other.

"It's good to see you out and about, Tom."

"I'm sure it is, Dan," Wilmot said. "My friend Canyon here told me how concerned you were for me."

"Uh, yeah, that's right."

"He told me you didn't want him coming out to the ranch to see me, Dan," Wilmot said. "Why was that, Dan?"

"Well . . . like I said, Tom, I was concerned about you. I didn't know who he was, and I didn't want him bothering you."

"He doesn't bother me, Dan," Wilmot said. "Canyon O'Grady is probably the best friend I have, right now—the *only* friend, in fact."

"That's not true, Tom," Dan Fisher said. "You have a lot of friends."

"Sure I do," Tom Wilmot said, "like all the friends who have been coming out to see me and Olivia. Oh, yeah, I forgot, you're all so busy."

"Tom—"

"Forget it, Dan," Wilmot said. "I just stopped in to see how you were doing, to see how you were enjoying my job, and my desk—"

"It's my job now, Tom," Fisher said. "I was appointed by the town council to replace you."

"That's right," Wilmot said, "you were appointed, not elected. Well, we'll find out whose job it is when the next election comes around in a few months."

"The next election?" Fisher said. "Tom, you can't seriously expect to run for sheriff in the next election."

"I can't?" Wilmot said. "You just watch me."

With that Wilmot turned and stalked out of the office, followed by O'Grady, who had not said a word to Fisher the whole time.

Outside he caught up to Wilmot as he was crossing the street and said, "I didn't know you were intending to run for sheriff again."

"I know," Wilmot said, "neither did I."

They decided to stop in Boone's for a drink before heading back to the general store. As they entered the saloon together they drew looks from the other customers, as well as from Boone himself.

"As I live and breathe," Boone said as they both approached the bar, "Tom Wilmot."

"Hello, Boone."

"What'll you have, gents?"

"Beer?" Tom said to Canyon, who nodded. "Two beers, Boone."

"Comin' up," Boone said.

He set the two mugs down in front of them and asked, "What brings you to town, Tom?"

"Came to say hello to all my old friends, Boone," Wilmot said, picking up his mug."

"Oh," Boone said. Someone at the other end of the bar banged on it for service and Boone said, " 'Scuse me."

"Is Boone one of your old friends?" Canyon asked.

"Boone doesn't have any friends," Wilmot said. "He just runs his business. I'd never expect Boone to come out and see how I was doin'."

"That's good," Canyon said, "because I like him."

"Boone's all right," Wilmot said. "You know what to expect from him. He's not a phony like these others, claiming to be my friends and then stabbing me in the back by appointing Fisher sheriff."

"Just to act as devil's advocate a little, Tom," Canyon said, "they did have to appoint someone to replace you."

"Yeah, they did," Wilmot said, and then added, "temporarily. Once I was back on my feet they should have given me my job back—or don't you think I could do the job with one arm?"

"Take it easy, Tom," Canyon said. "I'm on your side, remember?"

The fiery look in Wilmot's eyes suddenly dimmed a bit and he said, "Jesus, I'm sorry, Canyon. I didn't mean to snap at you."

"It's all right. You did raise a valid question, but you asked the wrong person. What about the voters? Are they going to think that you can do the job with one arm?"

Wilmot thought that over and then said, "I don't know, Canyon. To tell you the truth *I* don't even know if I can do the job again."

"Well," Canyon said, "you don't have to run for office again, you know. I mean, you mentioned it only to Fisher, and no one else—"

"Oh, don't worry," Wilmot said, interrupting him, "Fisher will make sure that Abe, and Morris, and the others know I said it. I'm locked into it now, Canyon. Locked into running, anyway."

"What will Olivia say to that, Tom?"

"I don't know. I suppose we'll find out when I tell her, won't we?"

"I guess so."

After they left the saloon they split up. Wilmot went to the general store to check on the supplies. O'Grady had to go to the telegraph office to send another message to Rufus Wheeler—one that he knew his superior was not going to like getting.

After Tom Wilmot and Canyon O'Grady left his office Dan Fisher sat down behind his desk and thought about what Wilmot had said. There was no way the one-armed man could defeat him in an open election for sheriff, was there? Surely by now people had forgotten Sheriff Tom Wilmot, and if he did run he sure wouldn't be the *same* Tom Wilmot.

Fisher decided to go and talk the situation over with Abe Gorman.

When Tom Wilmot came within sight of the general store he saw Dan Fisher coming out. He could have confronted the man, but he decided not to. He had figured that Fisher would go to Gorman anyway, so there was no point in bracing the man. He waited until Fisher had gotten far enough away and then crossed the street to the store and entered. In passing the buckboard he saw that all of the supplies had been loaded.

"Supplies ready, Abe?" he called as he entered.

Gorman started behind the counter and stared at Wilmot.

"Oh, Tom," he said, "you, uh, startled me."

The man was still wearing the puzzled frown he must have adopted when Fisher told him that Wilmot was going to run for office again.

"Sure, the supplies are loaded," Gorman said. "Uh, here's your bill."

"Thanks," Wilmot said. "I'll pay it as soon as I can."

"Don't worry. Like I said, your credit is good here."

"Thanks, Abe."

"Sure."

Wilmot was almost out the door when he turned and asked perversely, "Is anything wrong, Abe?"

"Huh?" the preoccupied man said. "Oh, no, Tom, nothing, nothing at all."

"Oh," Wilmot said, "because you look like you've got something on your mind."

"Well," Gorman said, "you know, just things."

"Sure, things. I know."

Outside Wilmot saw O'Grady approaching.

After both Fisher and Wilmot had come and gone Abe Gorman decided to close the store for a while so he could think.

Tom Wilmot had been a very popular sheriff in Rayford for a lot of years, and for that reason Gorman had supported him. It was good for Gorman's own political career to do so. However, once Wilmot had been injured, Gorman had made the decision to go with Fisher as sheriff. He had championed Fisher to the other members of the council and had eventually gotten them over to his side.

Now if Wilmot was considering running for sheriff, there could be a big problem there for Gorman. Even with his one arm, people would remember Wilmot, and some of them would even vote for him. Surely not enough to get him the job; after all, who wants a one-armed sheriff? Still, if Wilmot retained even a hint of his former popularity, it would not look good for Gorman to oppose him—and yet Gorman could not see himself supporting a one-armed man for sheriff.

Rayford would become the laughingstock of the country, and that would *not* be good for his political career.

There had to be a way out of this.

When Canyon left the telegraph office he knew he'd be getting a quick reply from Wheeler, but he decided not to wait around for it. He told the clerk that when the response did come he was to leave it at the hotel for him.

When he reached the general store he saw Wilmot standing by the buckboard.

"Ready to go?" Canyon asked.

"Yeah," Tom said, "but you ain't."

"What do you mean?"

"Get your stuff from the hotel," Wilmot said. "You'll be staying with us."

6

No amount of arguing would change Tom Wilmot's mind. Canyon told him he didn't want to impose on Olivia, but Wilmot assured him that Olivia was as much in favor of the offer as Wilmot himself was. The agent also pointed out that Tom and Olivia's relationship had suddenly taken a turn for the better, and he didn't want to be in their way, but Wilmot was still not having any and O'Grady finally agreed to move.

They took the buckboard over to the hotel, and Wilmot went inside with O'Grady.

"Mr. Wilmot," Erica Gardner said. She seemed pleased to see the ex-lawman. "How nice to see you."

"And you, Miss Gardner."

"How is Mrs. Wilmot?"

"She's fine, thank you."

"Please send her my best regards."

"I'll do that, Miss Gardner."

Erica turned her attention to Canyon then.

"Is there something I can do for you, Mr. O'Grady?" she asked.

"As a matter of fact there is. I'm afraid I'll be checking out."

"You don't like our hotel?"

"No, it's nothing like that," Canyon said. "The

hotel is fine—especially the service—but I have to leave—"

"I'm afraid this is my fault, Miss Gardner," Wilmot said, "mine and my wife's. You see, we've invited Canyon to be our house guest."

"I see," Erica said. "Well, that's certainly a good reason. I can't fault you for preferring Mrs. Wilmot's home cooking to that of our kitchen."

"You'll prepare my bill then?"

"There won't be any bill, Mr. O'Grady. After all, you never did use the room, did you?"

"Still," Canyon argued, "I *did* occupy it for a night, keeping you from renting it to someone else. I should pay for it."

"Please," she said, "I feel firmly about this. There won't be any bill."

"Well," O'Grady said with a sideways glance at Wilmot, "this seems to be my day for losing arguments. Thank you, Miss Gardner."

"Erica," she said, "please."

"I'll wait here while you get your gear," Wilmot said.

"Okay," Canyon said.

He went upstairs, collected his belongings, and came right back down. He had only been gone a few moments, and yet he had the distinct feeling that something had occurred in his absence.

"Good-bye, Miss—I mean, Erica."

"Mr. O'Grady," she said, "I hope you enjoy your stay."

"I'll enjoy it more if you'll call me Canyon next time we meet."

"Very well," she said, "next time we meet."

He nodded, smiled, and headed for the door.

"See you later tonight, Erica," he heard Tom say.

Outside Canyon stopped and said, "What do you mean you'll see her tonight?"

"So will you," his friend said. "I invited her to dinner."

"And what will Olivia think of that?"

Tom smiled—the first genuine smile Canyon had seen on the man's face since his arrival—and said, "She's going to love it."

"I love it," Olivia Wilmot said, clapping her hands together. "We're having company for dinner."

"Do you know Erica Gardner?" Canyon asked.

"Oh, yes," Olivia said, "we've talked in town many times." She looked directly at Canyon and said, "She's a wonderful girl."

"I'm sure." O'Grady could hardly believe that this was the same woman who had collapsed into his arms yesterday—twice.

They had unloaded the buckboard, with Wilmot doing what he could one-handed, and Olivia carrying what she could handle, and were now having a cup of coffee before continuing to work.

"There's, uh, another piece of news that will interest you," Tom said to Olivia.

"Oh, good," she said, "more news. What is it?"

Wilmot looked at O'Grady, who pointedly looked away and then asked, "Would you like me to leave?"

"No," Tom said, "there's nothing you can't hear."

Now Olivia lost her eager look and instead began to look concerned.

"What is it?" she asked. "Is something wrong?"

"No," Wilmot said, "depending on how you look at it."

"Tom Wilmot," she said, becoming firm now, "why

don't you just spit it out and I'll decide how I should look at it."

"I, uh, told Dan Fisher—"

"You saw Dan Fisher?" she snapped.

"That's right."

"I hope you gave him a piece of your mind—and mine!" she said fervently.

"Well . . . I gave him a piece of information."

"Such as?"

"I, uh, told him I'd be running against him in the next election."

She looked stunned for a moment, and then asked, "For what?"

"What do you mean, for what?" Wilmot asked. "For sheriff, of course."

She was silent again for a few seconds and then said, "You're insane." She looked at Canyon accusingly and said, "You let him do that?"

"It was out of his mouth before I knew it," Canyon said helplessly.

"Canyon had nothing to do with it, Olivia," Wilmot said. "It was my decision."

"Don't you think that was something we should have decided together?" she demanded.

"Yes," he said, "you're probably right—"

"I'm *probably* right?"

"Okay, you are right, and I'm sorry, but I can't back out now. I saw Fisher coming out of the general store. He's sure to have told Abe Gorman about it already."

"Well," she said, "it doesn't really matter."

"I'm going to run, Olivia," Wilmot said.

"I know you will, Tom," she said. "If you said you will, then you will, but it really doesn't matter."

"Why not?" Wilmot asked, frowning.

"Because," she said, very seriously, "you won't win. You *can't* win."

"I can't?"

"No."

"Why not?" he asked, his anger rising.

"No one will vote for a one-armed man for sheriff," she said. "It's as simple as that."

"You don't think I can do the job, do you?"

"That's not the point."

"Sure it is—" he said and stopped when Canyon grabbed his arm.

"Take it easy, Tom."

"Take it easy . . . " he muttered. "You talk to her, Canyon. I'm going for a walk."

"Tom—" Olivia said, but he was already out of the door and gone.

She turned to Canyon and said, "He's crazy, isn't he?"

"Olivia, it was just something he said, and now he feels he has to live up to it."

"But he'll do it," she said, "and it's madness."

"If you don't think he'll get elected," Canyon said, "why are you so upset?"

"What if he does get elected?" she asked. "Next time he'll get killed. I don't want to lose him just when we've found each other again, Canyon."

"Do you think this town would elect him, even with . . . without his arm?"

"I don't know," she said, "oh, I just don't know . . . but I'm afraid. You'll have to talk to him, Canyon. He'll listen to you."

"You think I can talk him out of this?"

"You have to *try*," she said, pleading. "Please, just try."

He took her hand and said, "I'll try, Olivia. I'll give it a try."

"Thank you." She pulled her hand from his and said, "Now get out of here. I have to get dinner ready."

"All right."

He stepped outside and took a quick look around. Wilmot was nowhere to be seen. He decided not to go looking for his friend, but to let him come back when he was ready.

He unhitched the team from the buckboard and took them into the livery. He rubbed them down and fed them, then went and saw to the buckboard. Wilmot still had not returned. There wasn't much that they could do today anyway, not until the lumber they had ordered was delivered in the morning, so he took a turn around the ranch, making mental notes on what work had to be done.

Canyon hoped Tom Wilmot would decide to return before their dinner guest arrived.

7

Tom Wilmot reappeared about a half an hour before Erica Gardner did. He did so quietly and went inside to wash up for dinner. Canyon had already gotten ready for dinner and was just waiting on the front porch. He was surprised at how much he was looking forward to Erica's appearance.

Behind him the front door opened and Olivia came out.

"How is he?" Canyon asked.

"Quiet," she said.

"Is this going to be a difficult dinner?" he asked. "Because if it is—"

"No, it'll be all right," Olivia said. "He's still a different man, Canyon. He'll be fine with Erica. You met her when you registered at the hotel?"

"That's right."

"Were you . . . impressed?" she asked with a grin.

"What do you think?"

Her grin widened into a smile.

"I'll bet you were," she said. "She's a lovely girl. You know why Tom invited her here, don't you?"

"Because you like playing cupid?" Canyon said.

"I should know better with you, though, shouldn't I?" she said. "Still like women, Canyon? Lots and lots of women?"

"Olivia—"

"Oh, that's right," she said, "*they* like you, don't they?"

"Olivia—"

"Not that I blame them, actually," she said, and Canyon started to become uncomfortable with the way she was looking at him. He knew that he liked women—yes, lots and lots of women—but he had never slept with the wife of a friend.

He turned and looked out from the house and breathed a sigh of relief when he saw the approaching rider. It was a few moments before he realized that it was Erica. For some reason he had expected her to arrive in a buggy.

"Company's here," he said.

"Good," she said. "You show her in. I'll go inside and make sure everything is . . . all right."

Before he could say anything she had gone back inside the house. He shrugged and stepped down off the porch to meet Erica.

As her horse reached him he held its head and then helped her to dismount. He ended up with his hands on her waist.

"Hello," he said.

"Hello."

She was a tall girl, just several inches shorter than he was. She was wearing boots, but even without them she would have been taller than was common.

"Let me take care of your horse," he said.

"Can I come?"

"Sure. Come on."

They walked to the stable together, not talking. Inside, while he unsaddled her horse she said, "I'm glad I was invited. Was it your idea?"

"No," he said, "or shouldn't I admit that?"

"No, it's all right," she said. "Actually, I didn't think it was your idea, but I thought I'd ask."

"What made you think it wasn't my idea?"

"You don't strike me as the kind of man who has other people set up his meetings with women."

"I'm not," he said, beginning to run the horse down a bit.

"I didn't think so."

She moved up next to him and when he turned to look at her she put her arms around him and kissed him. Her mouth was at once soft and insistent. Her tongue slithered into his mouth and he put his hands on her waist again. This time he grabbed her shirt and pulled it out of her pants, then slid his hands underneath it. Her cupped two firm, warm breasts and felt the nipples harden against his palms. He went down to his knees and pressed his mouth to her abdomen. Her flesh was hot against his lips. He worked his way up to her breasts, and when he took one of her nipples into his mouth and sucked it she whimpered and pushed him away.

"It's too rushed," she gasped. "They're waiting for us inside."

"You started it," he said, looking up at her from his knees.

She laughed and backed away from him, tucking in her shirt.

"You started it when you walked into my hotel," she said.

"Well," he said, getting to his feet and brushing off his knees, "I guess we'll finish it later. We'd better go in to dinner."

They walked together to the house, with a respectable distance between them. He was savoring the taste of her nipples, which was still on his tongue.

* * *

When they got inside Olivia greeted Erica warmly and gave them both a knowing look. Tom Wilmot was certainly pleasant to Erica, although on the whole throughout the meal he was rather quiet. Olivia carried the bulk of the conversation while Canyon and Erica tossed looks back and forth across the table. Once or twice Canyon felt a foot on his leg and was certain it belonged to Erica. At least he *hoped* it belonged to Erica. He would have hated to think that it belonged to Olivia. No, that was unthinkable.

After dinner Olivia served coffee, and when it came time for Erica to leave it was dark out.

"I'd better ride back to town with Erica, Olivia," Canyon said.

"Of course, Canyon," she said. "Be careful, though."

"Sure." On the way out he said, "See you later, Tom," to Wilmot.

"Yeah," Wilmot said, "sure."

While he was saddling Cormac and Erica's horse she said, "Mr. Wilmot was very quiet this evening."

"Yes, he was."

"Is there something wrong?"

He looked at her and said, "He and Olivia just need some time together to talk some things over."

"Oh, I see," she said. "Do you think that escorting me back to town and then riding back will give them time enough?"

He stared at her for a moment and said, "No, I don't."

When they returned to town they left their animals at the livery and he followed her to the hotel. She used her key to let them in through the back door, and then she led him down a hallway to her room.

Once inside she turned and kissed him the way she had in the Wilmot stable. This time when he pulled her shirt out of her pants and started mouthing her nipples, she didn't push him away. Instead she peeled the shirt off and discarded it, then reached down and pulled his off over his head without even unbuttoning it.

While on his knees he removed her boots and loosened her britches and pulled them down so she could kick them away. He pulled her panties down then and even before she could kick them away his mouth was on her, his tongue probing. She gasped and her knees almost gave right there and then. She put her hands on his shoulders and leaned on him while he worked her with his mouth.

"Oh, God, yes," she moaned, "Jesus, yes, right there . . ."

He felt her legs begin to tremble and then she cried out. He stood and lifted her in his arms, carried her to the bed. Waves of pleasure were still coursing through her as he removed his own boots and pants and then joined her on the bed.

He tried to mount her, but she reversed their positions with surprising strength and straddled him. She took hold of his rigid cock and then lowered herself down onto it, taking him inside of her, which is where they were now.

Erica Gardner's breasts were full and round, the nipples and aureola dark brown. O'Grady palmed them while she rode him up and down. As she tossed her head he admired the smoothness of her long neck. Her hands were pressed down on his belly and as she lifted herself up on him all her weight was centered there, and then she'd let herself drop down on him, driving him home to the hilt inside of her.

She continued to ride him, her tempo increasing, and then she was bouncing up and down on him so energetically that her breasts were bouncing. He could see that she was biting her lower lip so hard that she might even bite through it.

He put his hands on her hips and began to lift his butt off the bed every time she came down on him, which made him penetrate her even more . . . if that was possible.

He could feel his orgasm welling up inside of him, driving up his legs and through his loins until suddenly he exploded into her with manic intensity. She opened her mouth as if to scream, but no sound came out. He groaned aloud and she fell on him, her breasts pressed tightly to his chest and her mouth covering his. They continued to ride the great waves of pleasure, their mouths pressed firmly together, muffling their cries . . .

"My father is in the room next door," she muttered against his mouth just moments later. "We mustn't make too much noise."

"Now you tell me," he said.

She slid off of him and lay beside him, one hand still resting on his hip.

"I'm sorry," she said, "I meant to tell you, but I was just in such a *hurry* to get you in here—to get you in *me*."

"I know. I felt the same way."

"I felt it that very first day," she said. "I wanted to grab you and drag you back here and tear your clothes off. Is that wicked of me to admit?"

"No," he said, "it's honest, and there's nothing wicked about being honest."

She slid her hand over his hip and rested it on his belly, just above his pubic hair.

"Will you be staying around Rayford much longer?" she asked.

"A few days, at least," he said, "maybe more."

"To help Mr. Wilmot?"

"If I can."

"Do you think you'll have any . . . time for me? I mean, do you think we can . . . uh, do this again . . . some time?"

He slid his hand onto her belly now and said, "I think we'll be able to do this again . . . and again . . . and again—as many times as you like."

She smiled and moved her hand, taking hold of his semi-erect penis.

"Tonight?"

He turned to her, taking her into his arms, and said, "We can try."

"But quietly," she warned him, her mouth pressed to his neck, "quietly . . . "

8

In the morning while they were getting dressed Erica said, "I hope the Wilmots had enough time to work out their differences."

"I think we gave them enough time, don't you?" Canyon asked.

"Well," she said, "if not, you can always come back."

He smiled and said, "I'll keep that in mind."

"You'll have to go out the back way," she said, moving to the door. "Just let me check the hall."

He waited while she opened the door, stuck her head out, and looked both ways.

"Okay," she said, "the coast is clear. Come on."

She stepped out into the hall and he followed her to the back door. Before she let him out she kissed him warmly and he put one arm around her and pulled her close to him.

"I'll see you when I come back to town," he promised.

"I'll be waiting," she said.

As he stepped out she said, "Oh, I forgot. Yesterday a telegraph message came for you. I'm keeping it behind the desk."

He stopped and thought for a moment. The message could only be from Wheeler, and it was probably telling him to get his ass back to Washington.

"I'll pick it up," he said to her, "next time I'm in town."

As he rode up to the Wilmot house Canyon saw Olivia standing outside.

"Good morning," she greeted him.

"How's Tom this morning?"

"He's fine," she said. "How's Erica?"

"She's great."

"I'll bet."

Canyon dismounted and started leading Cormac to the stable.

"I've got coffee on," she said, "and Tom's about to get up. He wants to talk to you."

"I'll be right in."

He unsaddled Cormac, cared for him and then went back to the house. When he entered he saw Tom Wilmot sitting at the kitchen table.

"Guess I made a fool of myself last night . . . again," Wilmot said.

"If you did nobody noticed," Canyon said, sitting down across from his friend.

Olivia brought Canyon a cup of coffee and gave him a look that said, "Oh no?"

"Look, Canyon," Wilmot said, "we have to talk."

"About what?"

"If I'm gonna get my job back I'm gonna need your help."

"I'm here, Tom. But are you sure that's what you want to do?"

Wilmot exchanged a glance with Olivia, and then said, "Yeah, it's what I want."

"Then how do you propose we go about it?"

"Well, first," Wilmot said, "I need to learn to shoot with my left hand. That's where you come in."

"How?"

"If I remember correctly, you shoot just as well with either hand."

"I shoot fairly well left-handed. So?"

"So you're gonna teach me."

"So you learn to shoot left-handed? So what? How does that get you voted in as sheriff?"

"It doesn't," Wilmot said, "but it prepares me to prove to the townspeople that I can do the job."

"And how are you going to do that?"

Wilmot leaned forward and said, "There's only one way I'm going to prove to them that I can still do the sheriff's job."

"And how is that?" Canyon asked again.

"I'm going to find the men who shot me and bring them back."

Canyon hesitated a moment and then said, "What?" He looked at Olivia, but she shrugged and looked away. Apparently, Wilmot had convinced her to go along with his plan.

"Tom, you were shot—what, seven months ago? The men who shot you are long gone."

"If they're still in this country," Wilmot said, "I'll find them."

"But you don't even know who they are," Canyon said. When Wilmot did not immediately reply Canyon said, "Or do you?"

"I recognized two of them," Wilmot said after a moment. "I saw them standing over me."

"And you never told anyone?"

"No."

"Why not?"

"At first," Wilmot said, "it didn't matter. I just didn't care. Later, I figured I'd just keep the information to myself in case I could use it. Now I know that I have to find them and bring them back."

"He can't do it alone, Canyon," Olivia said.

"I know that, Olivia," O'Grady said.

"I need your help," Wilmot said. "I need you to go with me."

Canyon's first thought was of Rufus Wheeler. He wouldn't take *this* turn of events very well.

"Will you help me?"

"If this is really what you want to do, Tom, of course I'll help you. You're my friend."

"That's good," Wilmot said, "because even if you didn't help me I'd do it without you."

"I know you would." Canyon looked at Olivia and asked, "What do you think about all this?"

"I think it's crazy," she said, "but if he's gonna do it, I'm happy that you'll be with him."

"To help me," Wilmot said to one or both of them. He wasn't looking at either of them, but down at his coffee cup. "To help me," he repeated, and then added, "not to take care of me."

"Of course," Olivia said. "To help you."

There was an awkward silence then and Canyon decided to break it before it went on too long.

"And that help starts now," he said, standing up. "Get your gun, Tom. Let's see what you can do left-handed."

Olivia's contribution to the proceedings was an array of empty bottles and cans. O'Grady and Wilmot took them behind the barn where the redhaired agent set them up on a fence. Olivia did not stay around to watch.

Canyon stood next to Tom Wilmot, who had his gun stuck in his belt.

"Let me see that," Canyon said.

Wilmot handed O'Grady the gun. He inspected it, then stuck it into his own belt and handed Wilmot his own gun.

"Use mine," he said. "Yours needs a good cleaning."

Wilmot started to tuck the gun into his belt.

"Keep it in your hand," Canyon said. "I don't want to see how fast you can draw it, just how well you can shoot it."

"All right."

"Take the cans first."

Canyon had set the bottles and cans up so that they stood can, bottle, can, bottle—every other one being a can or a bottle.

"All right."

Wilmot extended his hand, holding the gun straight out, and jerked the trigger. One of the bottles shattered.

"I hit one," Wilmot said.

"A bottle," Canyon said. "I said hit a can."

"I didn't think you'd notice."

"Unless you're fooling around and meant to hit the bottle."

"No," Wilmot said, honestly, "I was aiming for the can to the right of that bottle."

"Okay, then," Canyon said, "try it again, and squeeze the trigger, don't jerk it."

Wilmot emptied the gun without striking a can *or* another bottle.

"I see we have our work cut out for us," Canyon said, taking the gun back. He ejected the spent shells and loaded in six live rounds. He then holstered the gun. "There's something else we have to deal with, as well," he said.

"What's that?"

"Your physical condition."

Wilmot bristled and said, "Nothing much I can do about that, is there?"

"Don't be so goddamned sensitive," Canyon said. "We're not going to get anywhere if you take offense at everything I say."

Wilmot backed off immediately and said, "You're right. Sorry."

"I'm talking about your being in the kind of physical condition a manhunt will demand. We're going to have to build you up, build up your strength and stamina."

"I see," Wilmot said. "And how are we going to do that?"

"In the most productive way I can think of," Canyon said. "By fixing this place up."

As if on cue they both heard the sound of a wagon. They came out from behind the barn and saw a buckboard delivering the lumber they had bought yesterday in town.

Over the course of the next couple of weeks they worked around the ranch during the day, and worked on Wilmot's shooting after dinner, while it was still light. During that time Canyon made as many trips into town as he could to be with Erica, whose father eventually started to suspect what was going on.

The other thing Canyon had to do was send another telegram to Rufus Wheeler, asking for what amounted to a leave of absence from duty. It took quite a few exchanges for him to properly explain the situation, but in the end Wheeler agreed. In his last message, however, he did mention that O'Grady would have some heavy paying back to do. O'Grady knew the man was serious, too.

In the evenings, after the ranch work had been done, and the shooting lesson was over, they would sit around and discuss how they would go about the manhunt.

Tom Wilmot identified two of the men who had shot him as the January brothers, Sam and Carl.

"I never had any dealings with them before," he told Canyon, "but I saw enough paper on them to know it was them."

"Do we know who they run with?" Canyon asked.

"No," Wilmot said, "but we can find out. I still have some friends around—at least, I hope I do."

They sent out a ton of telegraph messages to friends they both had. They were asking for any information on the whereabouts of the January brothers, and any information on who they rode with, either presently, or back when they had shot Wilmot down.

While they continued to build up both Wilmot and the ranch, they collected information little by little. They would put it all together until they felt they had enough material to use to launch a manhunt.

The other thing they had to decide was whether or not they would hunt for these men alone, or enlist help. They each knew of several people they could ask for help, but it was Wilmot who resisted the idea.

"I have to prove to these people that I can do the job," he said, "and I can't have an army behind me. That won't prove anything."

"Maybe not," Canyon said, "but it might get us killed."

"We can wait on this question, can't we?" Wilmot said. "I mean, until we know what we're gonna do and when?"

"Sure," Canyon said, "it can wait, Tom . . . but

not too long. If we are going to bring in some help we're going to have to give them time to get here."

"We'll have time," Wilmot said. "Trust me."

"Do me a favor, Tom."

"What?"

"Don't say 'trust me.' "

9

Because his involvement with Tom Wilmot was on a personal level Canyon hesitated to telegraph Washington for assistance, but he finally relented when no useful information was forthcoming from other sources. He sent Wheeler a telegram asking for information on the whereabouts of a couple of outlaws by the name of the January brothers.

By the time they had effected repairs to the barn, the corral, and the house Wheeler's reply had arrived. It was delivered to the hotel by the telegraph operator, and Erica gave it to Canyon while they were in her bed.

"This came for you today," she said, handing it to him reluctantly.

He read it quickly, then folded it and put it on the table next to the bed.

"Is that the information you've been waiting for?" she asked.

"Yes."

"That means you'll be leaving soon."

"That's right."

She rolled over onto her side, turning her back to him. "I don't know why I feel like this," she said. "I knew this day was coming."

He touched her shoulder but she didn't respond.

"I have to go and tell Tom."

"So go ahead," she said, keeping her back to him. She didn't turn over while he dressed, nor when he was ready to leave.

"Erica—"

"Just remember to come and say good-bye before you leave," she said.

"I will."

He picked up the telegram and left.

When he reached the ranch Tom Wilmot was putting the finishing touches on some repairs to the porch. Over the course of the past few weeks Wilmot had become more and more adept at doing things one-handed. O'Grady was particularly impressed with the way the man was handling a gun left-handed.

As Canyon dismounted Wilmot stood up, setting the hammer down, and looked at him expectantly. The front door opened and Olivia came out.

Canyon mounted the porch and handed the telegram to Wilmot, who opened it and read it. Olivia didn't wait to find out what it said. She knew what it *meant*. She turned and went back inside.

"Texas," Wilmot said, looking at Canyon.

"Last place they were seen," the agent said. "It's a long way off. By the time we get there the trail will be cold."

"Maybe," Wilmot said, "but not eight months cold."

"No."

"When do you want to leave?" Wilmot asked.

"You're ramrodding this hunt, Tom," Canyon said. "It's your call."

"We'll have to outfit," Wilmot said.

"Are we getting help?"

"All this says is that the January brothers were seen," Wilmot said. "Doesn't say anything about anyone else. If it's just the two of them, we can handle it. If we run into trouble along the way we can get some help."

"If we get help it's got to be someone we can trust," Canyon said, "not just somebody we pick up along the way."

"I know that," Wilmot said. "Let's go it alone for now, Canyon."

He shrugged and said, "Like I said, it's your call."

"We can go into town today and outfit," Wilmot said, talking half to Canyon and half to himself, "and we can leave tomorrow."

"What about Olivia?"

Wilmot looked at O'Grady and said, "She's prepared for this, Canyon."

So was Wilmot himself, Canyon observed. Over the past three weeks the man had put on almost twelve pounds, and his stamina had improved threefold. Still, there was no telling how he would react to long hours on horseback until they actually started the trip. But he was far from the man Canyon had seen when he first arrived.

Olivia, too, had started to look better—physically, anyway. She had added some weight and no longer looked as if she were carrying the weight of the world on her shoulders, but there was still something different about her, something Canyon couldn't quite pinpoint. Maybe it was her eyes. They looked as if there was something going on behind them.

"You just rode in," Wilmot said. "I'll ride into town and buy what we need."

"I can go with you."

Wilmot gave O'Grady a look and said, "I can go alone, Canyon."

O'Grady decided not to argue. "Okay, Tom."

Wilmot went inside and came out wearing the new gun belt they had bought for him. "Still feels odd having this on my left hip," he said, plucking at it, "but I think I'm getting used to it."

They walked over to the barn together and Wilmot allowed O'Grady to saddle his horse for him, simply because it would be faster. He was unsaddling Cormac as Wilmot mounted up.

"I should be back in a few hours," Wilmot said.

"Whenever," Canyon said. "Just don't go looking for trouble."

"Me?" Wilmot said. "I never look for trouble, Canyon, but at least I know that—for the first time in months—if it comes, I can handle it."

"Just remember," Canyon said, "you can also walk away from it."

"Sure, partner," Wilmot said, "I'll remember."

Canyon couldn't help feeling that when Wilmot left he was on the prod, eager to show off his newfound left-handed abilities with his gun.

Canyon was finishing up with Cormac when he felt the presence of someone else in the barn. He turned and saw Olivia standing in the doorway, watching him. She was leaning against the wall with her right elbow, her arm above her head. She was hipshot, with one leg slightly bent. She was wearing a simple, high-necked dress and—from experience—Canyon could tell that she was wearing nothing underneath. The shape of her breasts, which had filled out some since he had arrived, were plainly visible beneath the thin material of her dress, and he could see the outline of her nipples. There was no denying Olivia Wilmot was a beautiful woman, and he felt a stirring that he didn't want to feel.

"Where's Tom?" she asked.

"He went to town to get us outfitted for the trip," Canyon said, turning his attention back to his horse.

"He won't be back for a while, then," she said.

He fed Cormac and then turned to face Olivia, who had stepped away from the wall and taken several steps toward him. It was plain to him now what she wanted. He could almost *smell* her readiness, and knew now that he hadn't been imagining things of late.

"What's going on, Olivia?"

"What do you mean?" She clasped her hands behind her back, a movement that thrust her breasts forward.

"You know what I mean," Canyon said. "Tom is my friend."

"And he's my husband," she said. "What's that got to do with anything?"

"Olivia—"

"Canyon," she said, moving closer still, "it doesn't matter, really. When you and Tom get back I'll be leaving him, anyway."

"What?"

"I've been wanting to leave him for a long time," she said, "but I couldn't, not when he was helpless, but now . . . now that he's a man again, I can do it."

"So then what's *this* about?" he asked.

"This?" she said, spreading her hands. "Let's just say this is about curiosity, or that I'm making up for lost opportunities."

"What lost opportunities?"

"Oh, come on, Canyon," she said. "Over the years I've seen how you look at me."

"I *never* led you to believe—"

"That you'd want me?" she asked. "Tell me that you wouldn't want me, if I wasn't married to Tom."

"That would be a different situation," he said.

"I don't think so," she said. She walked right up to him now and put one hand on his arm. "As far as I'm concerned Tom and I are finished."

"But still married."

She took her hand off his arm and pressed both hands to her own loins, then slowly moved them up her body until she was cupping her own breasts.

"I saw you," she said, her voice growing thick and husky.

"Saw me? Doing what?"

"I saw you in here with Erica, that first day, when she came for dinner."

He remembered when he and Erica had almost made love in the barn, but had stopped for fear of being discovered. Apparently, they *had* been discovered.

"You were able to resist her that day, Canyon," Olivia said, unbuttoning her dress, "but you won't be able to resist me."

"Olivia," he said, "don't do this," but even as he said it he realized his own voice had grown thick. Her dress was open to the waist now and he could see her flesh, smell the musky scent that was rising from her.

She pulled the dress down her shoulders so that her breasts popped free, and then she cupped them in her hands again, flicking at the nipples with her thumbs.

"Tom's idea of sex has always been to get his own satisfaction as soon as possible and then roll off me," she said. "I've *never* been satisfied, Canyon, never been fulfilled . . . not the way *you* could fulfill me."

"Olivia," he said, "I can't—"

"You want to," she said, and then moaned, "Oh, I want you to, Canyon . . . "

She pressed herself against him then, the way she had been pressed against him weeks earlier, sobbing. Then her body had felt frail, but now she felt firm and exciting . . . and hot, *incredibly* hot!

He felt her hand between them, touching his hardness.

"Ooh, and you want me, too, don't you, Canyon O'Grady?" she cooed.

She fell to her knees then and undid his pants. He felt rooted to the spot as she reached in and took out his rigid cock.

"Oh, God," she breathed, "I knew you'd be beautiful . . . "

She closed her eyes and pressed her cheek to him, caressing him with one hand on his cock and the other cupping his balls. Lasciviously she flicked her tongue out to taste him, slowly, tantalizing licking him up and down. He felt as if he were going to burst then and there. He wanted her badly, right then, and felt his anger rising because of his need.

"Mmmm," she said, opening her mouth and taking him inside. Her head began to move as she rode him up and down, sucking him wetly. He reached down and cupped her head, throwing his head back and closing his eyes. Tom Wilmot could have walked in on them at that moment and Canyon never would have known it.

"Oh, God," she murmured against him, her mouth still on him. With her hands she eased his pants down to his ankles and then began to caress his thighs, running her hands up and down his powerful legs. Finally she reached behind him to cup his buttocks and pull him to her, taking him even deeper into her mouth.

Suddenly he growled and opened his eyes. He was angry with her because he couldn't resist. He reached for her, pulled her from his cock and yanked her to her feet.

"You want it, Olivia?" he demanded. "Is this what you want?"

He turned with her and pushed her into one of the stalls. She fell onto the hay and stared up at him, her naked breasts heaving, her nostrils flaring, her tongue visible on her lips, still tasting him.

"Come on," she pleaded, "come *on*, Canyon!"

He went to her then, but as she reached for him he grabbed her and turned her over onto her knees. He wanted it now, just as badly as she did, but he was still guilty enough *not* to want to see her face—the face of his friend's wife. He reached down and flipped her dress up and over her back. He realized again that she was wearing no underwear. That made him want her even more, and *that* made him feel even guiltier.

He spread her legs more and then drove his stiff cock up between her legs into her cunt. She gasped at first, as if he had hurt her, and then she cried out, but not in pain. He grasped her hips and began pulling her toward him and thrusting forward at the same time.

"Is this it, Olivia?" he asked, driving into her. "Is this what you wanted?"

"Oh, yes, Canyon," she moaned aloud, "yes, this is what I want, this is what I've always wanted."

Damn you, he thought, directing it both at her and at himself. He stared down at her beautiful ass and knew he should stop now and leave her like this, but he also knew he couldn't stop, not now. He was beyond stopping.

From that point on he was almost mindless in the way he drove into her. She gasped and moaned and cried, and when he reached beneath her and grabbed her breasts and held them and squeezed them while he continued to fuck her from behind she screamed, and then screamed again when he exploded into her. . . .

10

Canyon left her there afterward and didn't go back to the house. He could still see her lying on the hay, her beautiful buttocks still exposed, and then in his mind's eye she turned over and stared up at him through glazed eyes.

"My God," she'd said just before he left her, "I never felt anything like that before in my life . . . "

He walked away from her without saying anything. He was still feeling angry, but he was also feeling ashamed of himself. He had just had sex with his friend's wife, and he wasn't sure how he was going to handle it. He certainly couldn't tell Tom about it. Would Olivia? And whether she did or didn't, how could he ride all the way to Texas with the friend he had betrayed?

He didn't think Olivia would tell her husband, though. She wanted to leave Tom Wilmot, but she didn't seem to want to hurt him, otherwise she would have left him long ago. Canyon didn't want to hurt his friend, either, not when he was so recently recovered from his wounds, both physical *and* mental.

Canyon decided that he would just go ahead with the plans as they stood until Wilmot himself changed his mind—for whatever reason.

He continued walking, thinking now about what he

and Tom Wilmot had to do. He knew that bringing in the men who had shot him would do wonders for Wilmot's self-worth, but he seriously doubted that it would get the man elected sheriff of Rayford—or anyplace else, for that matter. It had nothing to do with his ability to do the job, it was just unlikely that any town would elect a one-armed man as their sheriff. O'Grady hoped that Wilmot would be able to deal with that when this was all over—not to mention dealing with his wife's leaving him.

Jesus, Canyon thought, he hoped his friend would be strong enough to deal with that.

When Canyon returned to the house he saw smoke coming from the chimney. Olivia was probably starting lunch, or possibly dinner. He decided to stay outside the house and finish some chores while waiting for Wilmot to return.

After a couple of hours of working he was taking a break when Olivia came out of the house. She walked over to him, carrying a cup.

"I thought you might be able to use a cup of coffee," she said, handing it to him.

"Thanks," he said, accepting it.

He expected her to say something and was surprised when she turned and walked away. She had not even looked directly into his eyes. She had treated him as if he was just a ranch hand.

Canyon O'Grady didn't think he would ever understand women.

When Wilmot returned, he didn't return alone. O'Grady saw the two riders approaching, leading two pack horses. He was then surprised when he recognized the other man.

It was Sheriff Dan Fisher.

Canyon put down the shovel he was holding, retrieved his gun belt, and stepped forward to meet them with it slung over his shoulder.

"Sheriff," Canyon said. "I'm surprised to see you here."

"I guess you are," Fisher said.

O'Grady looked at Wilmot, who hadn't said a word yet, but who was sitting his horse as if he was very proud of himself.

"What's going on?" Canyon asked.

"Maybe we should talk about it inside," Fisher said, "over coffee."

"We better see to your horses, first."

"I'll help you," Fisher said. "It'll give Tom time to talk to Olivia."

Wilmot handed his reins to O'Grady, dismounted, and walked to the house.

Fisher dismounted and walked to the barn with O'Grady, leading the four horses.

"Talk to Olivia about what?"

"I've been invited to dinner."

"Is that a fact?" Canyon asked. "By who? Yourself?"

"You could put it that way."

"How did you get Tom to agree to that?"

"I made a trade with him."

"And what did you have to offer?"

Fisher looked at O'Grady as they reached the barn and said, "I didn't put him in jail."

"Jail? For what?"

Inside the barn they stopped walking and faced one another.

"He killed a man."

"What?" Canyon said in surprise.

"He went into the saloon for a drink. This is what

I believe happened. He waited for someone to make a remark, possibly about his missing arm, and then he shot him down."

"But . . . why?"

"To prove a point, I think. Wouldn't you think so?" Fisher asked. "After all, aren't you the one who's been working with him so he could shoot left-handed?"

"I guess I am," Canyon said, "but I didn't think he'd do . . . that."

"Oh," Fisher said, "I'm sure he was provoked, but I'm also sure he might have been able to walk away from it—and once he would have."

"So why isn't he in jail? Surely not just because he invited you to dinner."

"No, but I'll be going along with you after the January brothers, and the others."

Surprised again Canyon said, "Is that a fact?"

"Don't tell me you don't think you can use another gun, Mr. O'Grady."

"Oh, we can use another gun, all right, Sheriff," Canyon said. "I just never expected it to be yours."

"Well, I never did, either."

"Let's get these animals taken care of," Canyon said. "I've got to get washed up before dinner."

Ironically, Canyon ended up putting Tom Wilmot's horse into the very stall where, just hours before, he had been pounding into the man's wife from behind.

They unloaded the pack animals and stowed the gear.

"We'll ride through town in the morning and pick up the food we need for the trip," Fisher said.

"We'll be leaving early."

"I talked to Abe Gorman," Fisher said. "He'll be waiting for us."

"Gorman, eh? Your coming along with us, that wouldn't be Gorman's idea, would it?"

"Why would it?"

"Well, I doubt Gorman would want Tom to run for sheriff and win, not after they handed his job to you. It wouldn't look good for you if Tom came back with the men who robbed the Rayford bank, would it?"

"I admit that's why I'm going," Fisher said. "I've got the job now, and I want to keep it. Is that a crime?"

"No, not a crime."

"And it was my idea, nobody else's."

"Well," Canyon said, "I can't say I'm not happy to have another gun along. How are you and Tom going to get along?"

"We'll do fine," Fisher said.

On the way back to the house Fisher said, "Speaking of getting along, how have you been getting along with Olivia?"

"Just fine," Canyon said, perhaps too quickly. "Why do you ask?"

Fisher shrugged, and O'Grady put his hand on the man's arm to stop him.

"What's on your mind?"

"Nothing."

"Something is," Canyon said. "Come on, tell me before we go inside."

"I was just wondering about you . . . and Olivia."

"Wondering what?"

"Take it easy, O'Grady," Fisher said. "I know how Olivia is, from experience."

"Are you saying that you and Olivia—"

"That's right," Fisher said. "She came to me while Tom was laid up, said she needed to be with somebody."

"And she picked you?"

"Why not?" Fisher asked. "I'm younger, I've got two arms, and by that time I was sheriff."

"How long did it go on?"

The man shrugged again and said, "A couple of months."

"And then what happened?"

"Then she took Tom home and told me it was all over," Fisher said.

Canyon thought it over for a moment, then asked, "Why are you telling me this?"

"I just . . . wanted to find out if there was anything between you and Olivia."

"No, she's married."

"And if she wasn't?"

O'Grady stared at Fisher a moment and then said, "You're in love with her, aren't you?"

"So?"

"You think she's going to leave Tom for you?"

"She'll leave him," Fisher said. "They weren't getting along that great *before* he was hurt. Once he's back on his feet, so to speak—"

"You can't lose, can you, Fisher?" Canyon said. "If he becomes sheriff, you figure you get Olivia, and if he doesn't, you get to keep the job."

Fisher didn't comment, except to say, "Dinner must be getting cold."

"Tell me something, Fisher," Canyon said, "which would you prefer, Olivia or the job?"

"Right now," Fisher said, "I think I'd prefer dinner."

11

Dinner was tense. There was tension between Canyon and Olivia, tension between Wilmot and Fisher, some between Wilmot and Olivia, to a lesser degree between Canyon and Fisher. Only because Fisher told him about his relationship with Olivia did Canyon see the tension between them, too. The only situation that didn't generate tension—anymore—was Canyon and Wilmot.

After dinner Canyon walked Fisher outside.

"We'll be leaving here at first light," Canyon said.

"I'll be ready when you reach town," Fisher said. "I'll saddle my own horse."

Canyon watched Fisher walk to the barn, and then Wilmot came out the door and stood next to him.

"What happened, Tom?"

"I cut a deal," Wilmot said. "It kept me out of jail, and got us another gun."

"Fisher's?"

"Sure, why not?" Wilmot said. "He was my deputy, remember? He's a good man when the lead is flying."

Fisher came riding out of the barn at that point and headed for town.

"What happened in town today?"

Wilmot shrugged and said, "Cowboy got out of hand."

"And you killed him?"
Wilmot continued to look straight ahead, at the steadily diminishing form of Dan Fisher—or maybe he was just looking in that direction.
"And you killed him?"
"I told him to stop," Wilmot said, "and he wouldn't."
"I thought you were going to walk away from trouble, Tom."
Wilmot turned his head and looked at O'Grady.
"I gave *him* the chance to walk away, Canyon," Wilmot said. "I gave him a choice, and he made it."
"Tom—"
"I'm gonna check my horse, make sure he's sound for the trip," Wilmot said, stepping down off the porch.
Canyon was about to follow him when Olivia came out and stood next to him. "Let him go," she said.
"He killed a man today, Olivia."
"I know."
"He did it just to prove a point."
"I know that, too."
He looked at her and said, "I don't know that I did the right thing, now. Teaching him to shoot left-handed, I mean."
"So? What are you gonna do now? Not go with him? He'll get killed, and then how will you feel?"
"I don't know," Canyon said, "how would you feel?"
"What do you mean?"
"If he died and didn't come back, you wouldn't have to leave him."
"Just because I want to leave him doesn't mean I want him dead, Canyon. That's unfair."
"Yeah, maybe."

"You're angry with me because of what happened today," she said, "Because you *enjoyed* what happened between us, just like I did."

Canyon looked at her and said, "Like you enjoyed yourself with Dan Fisher?"

She frowned and said, "Dan told you?"

"Yes."

"He had no right."

"He's in love with you."

"Well, I'm not in love with him."

"No?"

"No," she said. "Dan was just . . . there when I needed someone, that's all."

"And me?" he asked. "Was I just there?"

"No," she said, "I *wanted* you. I think I've always wanted you . . . but that doesn't mean I love you. If we're going to talk about love, I love Tom more than you *or* Fisher. If we're going to talk about lust, I want you more than either of them."

"You can forget that, Olivia," he said. "That will never happen again."

"Really?" she said, putting her hand on his hip briefly. "We'll see about that, won't we?"

She went back inside, and Canyon stayed on the porch a few minutes before heading for the barn himself. Checking Cormac over before the trip wasn't a bad idea.

In the barn Wilmot was bending over, checking his horse's hooves. He looked over his shoulder when O'Grady entered.

"Just checking my horse," Canyon said.

As Canyon starting checking over Cormac Wilmot straightened up. "Look, Canyon, maybe I made a mistake today," he said while O'Grady checked his horse's legs. "Maybe I overreacted."

"You call killing a man because he called you a name overreacting?"

"So I made a mistake," Wilmot said again, "but you should have seen the way those men in the saloon looked at me. At *me*, not at my missing arm."

Canyon imagined that must have made Wilmot feel good, for a change. He guessed he might also understand how Wilmot felt, but that still didn't make what the other man had done right. Then again, what about him? What he had done with Olivia wasn't right, either.

"How's your horse?" Wilmot asked.

"He's fine," Canyon said. "Yours?"

"He'll do," Wilmot said, slapping the animal's rump.

They faced each other.

"So what do we do now?" Canyon asked.

"Why don't we forget what's happened so far and start over from tomorrow," Wilmot suggested.

For a moment O'Grady wondered if Wilmot somehow knew what had happened between him and Olivia, but it was unlikely that the man would be so forgiving if he did.

"All right, Tom," Canyon said, "we'll start tomorrow."

As he had since his arrival Canyon bedded down near the fireplace. In all the time he'd slept there he'd never been disturbed. On this night he heard a door creak, and some floorboards. He looked up from the floor and saw Olivia standing there.

"What's wrong?"

"Did I wake you?"

"No. Is Tom all right?"

"He's fine," she said. "I can't sleep. I was going to make some tea—if it wouldn't disturb you."

"No, go ahead."

He moved so she could heat the water in the fireplace, and then she sat at the table with her tea.

"Why can't you sleep, Olivia?"

She didn't answer.

"Feeling guilty?" he asked.

"Guilty?" she asked, looking at him. "No, I don't feel guilty, Canyon. Not about anything. I gave as much as I had to give to Tom. I've got nothing to feel guilty about."

"Then why can't you sleep?"

She turned in her chair so she was facing him. She still hadn't touched her tea.

"I'll tell you why," she said. "I'm worried."

"About what?"

"About Tom. I don't want him getting killed trying to prove himself to a bunch of people who probably won't vote for him anyway."

"Maybe they're not who he's trying to prove himself to."

"What do you mean?"

"I mean maybe he's trying to prove himself to you, Olivia."

"Oh, no," she said. "I told you I don't feel guilty about anything, and you're not going to make me. It's more likely he's trying to prove something to himself."

Canyon couldn't argue with that because he'd thought of that himself.

Olivia got up and left the cup of tea on the table.

"Canyon, you've got to take care of him," she said. "Make sure he comes back alive."

"I'm going with him to help him, Olivia," Canyon said, "not to take care of him."

"Whatever you want to call it, Canyon," Olivia said. "Just watch out for him."

When Olivia got back into bed Tom Wilmot stirred and asked, "What's wrong?"

"Nothing, Tom," she whispered, "nothing at all. Go back to sleep."

She breathed a sigh of relief when he did as she asked rather than try to make love to her. His sex drive had returned these past three weeks, but the plain truth was that sex with Tom Wilmot had always been nothing more than a wifely duty to Olivia.

The quicker Tom and Canyon left and returned in one piece, the quicker she could break the news to Tom that she wanted to go and make a life for herself . . . alone.

After Olivia had gone back to bed Canyon thought about what she'd said. Of course, the plan was for him to go along with Wilmot on an equal basis, but when you trotted out the idea and looked at it plain, Tom Wilmot had only one arm. Chances were that Canyon *would* have to watch out for him along the way—that is, until Wilmot proved he could look after himself, which took more than shooting some mouthy drunk in a saloon.

For the first time since he found out that Dan Fisher was going along he was truly grateful for the lawman's presence.

12

Even before first light O'Grady and Wilmot had loaded up the pack horses and saddled their mounts. They were ready to leave when Olivia came out of the house.

"Be right back," Wilmot said to Canyon.

The agent watched as the man walked to his wife and put his lone arm around her, hugging her good-bye. Over Wilmot's shoulder Olivia was looking at Canyon.

He mounted up and waited for Wilmot to stop saying good-bye. The ex-lawman walked over and climbed aboard his horse with some difficulty. Beyond him Olivia waved to Canyon, who waved back after a second or two of hesitation.

"Good luck," she called out.

"We're gonna need it," Wilmot said to Canyon.

"I know," Canyon said. "Let's go."

In town Dan Fisher and Abe Gorman were in Gorman's general store, talking while Gorman put together the supplies the three men would be taking with them.

"This is a good idea, Dan, believe me," Gorman said. "You go along with them on this hunt and you can't lose. If you bring back any of the men, you'll look at least as good as Tom. If you fail—well, you won't lose anything. You might even gain some admiration for being willing to go outside your jurisdiction."

"I know all of this, Abe," Fisher said, but Gorman wasn't listening to anything but the sound of his own voice.

"And if Wilmot should happen to get killed," he was saying, "so much the better. In fact—"

He was cut off when Fisher grabbed the front of his shirt in both hands and pulled the man right up to him.

"What are you suggesting, Abe? That I kill Tom somewhere along the way?"

"I'm just saying it wouldn't hurt us if he didn't come back, Dan," Gorman said. He was trying to break free but could not.

"And then I'd have to kill O'Grady too, right?" Fisher went on. "Well, I'm not going along on this to kill anyone, Abe, unless it's those yahoos who robbed the bank and shot Tom."

Abruptly, Fisher let Gorman go, sending the man staggering across the room.

"Jesus . . ." Gorman said. "Dan, I wasn't suggesting that you kill anyone."

"That's good, Abe, real good," Fisher said. "Now get the rest of those supplies together. O'Grady and Tom will be here any time, now."

When O'Grady and Wilmot rode into town they went directly to the general store and found Dan Fisher waiting for them outside.

"Supplies are inside," Fisher said. "We can fit them on these pack horses."

"I'll go inside and help bring them out," Canyon said, dismounting. He was pleased that Wilmot didn't complain that he was being excluded because he had one arm.

Canyon went inside with Fisher, where Abe Gorman was waiting behind the counter. The supplies—coffee, beef jerky, flour, canned goods—were stacked on the counter next to Gorman.

"Nice of you to open early to accommodate us, Mr. Gorman," Canyon said.

"I'm just tryin' to help, Mr. O'Grady."

"Yeah," Canyon said, hefting a sack of flour up onto his shoulder. Fisher picked up some of the other supplies. At that moment they all heard shots from outside. Canyon dropped the sack of flour to the floor and ran for the door. He heard the other supplies drop to the floor as Fisher followed him.

As Canyon went out the door, lead chewed up the wall next to him. He dove for cover, pulling his gun from his holster. Behind him Fisher dove the other way, also drawing his gun.

"What the hell is going on?" Canyon shouted.

Down in the street Tom Wilmot was crouched behind a horse trough. Their horses had either run off, or Tom had run them off when the shooting started.

"Tom?" Canyon called out. "Do you know anything about this?"

Wilmot turned and said, "I might—"

There was a barrage of gunfire that cut their conversation short. They weathered the storm until the assailants stopped firing.

"What do you mean 'you might'?" Canyon asked.

"Well . . . I think they were with that fella I shot yesterday."

"How many we talking about?"

"Near as I can figure, four. They're all in doorways across the street."

"Sheriff!" Canyon called.

"I heard, O'Grady."

"Where are your deputies?"

"It's early," Fisher said, as if that explained it.

"So we have to get out of this by ourselves?" Canyon said.

"Why not?" Wilmot asked. "Might as well find out now if we can work together or not."

"Right," Canyon said, and the firing started again. This time the three men returned fire. The sound of breaking glass leaped into the air with the sound of shots, flying lead striking wood and glass—but not flesh. Not yet, anyway.

"You men!" Sheriff Fisher called out when the shooting stopped. "This is the sheriff. Throw down your guns and step out. You're all under arrest."

This was met with another barrage of gunfire. This time O'Grady, Wilmot, and Fisher preserved their lead.

"Well," Wilmot said when silence once again fell over the land, "that worked pretty good."

"Sheriff," Canyon called. When Fisher looked over at him Canyon pointed to himself and indicated that he was going to go back into the store. Fisher knew this meant that he would be going out the back door, and nodded.

Wilmot turned and nodded to Canyon. The agent moved while Wilmot and Fisher laid down some covering fire.

Inside the store Abe Gorman was crouched down behind his counter. The floor was strewn with shattered glass and broken stock.

"What's going on?" Gorman asked.

"Where's the back door?"

"There isn't any back door," Gorman said, "but there's a window in the stockroom."

"Stay down," Canyon said, and he didn't have to tell the storekeeper twice.

Canyon found the back window and climbed out. He worked his way along the back of the building until he reached an alley. He followed the alley to the main street and found himself a half a block away from where the shooting was still going on. There was a lull in the action just then, and he waited until it started up again to cross the street.

When he reached the other side he found that was where Wilmot's horse was and decided to stop. He slid his friend's rifle from the saddle and holstered his handgun. He moved into a doorway and stared down the street. From this vantage point he could see the four men who were still shooting at Wilmot and Fisher.

He had a choice. He could call out to them and give them a chance to surrender, or he could simply fire at them, probably taking out one or even two before they knew what was going on. He thought about warning them, but after all, they *were* bushwhackers. They fired at unsuspecting targets from cover, and that made them cowards. There was only one thing they would understand.

He lifted the rifle to his shoulder, sighted on the nearest man, and fired. As the man spun away beneath the impact of the bullet, he moved the barrel of the rifle and fired again.

As the second man fell, the other two stood up to see where the crossfire was coming from. Wilmot stood up at that point and fired. Fisher stepped into the street and fired his gun, and all four of the bushwhackers were dead.

Wilmot and Fisher crossed the street and met up with O'Grady to inspect the bodies.

"All dead," Fisher said.

"We make a good team after all," Wilmot said.

Fisher looked around, then at Canyon. "I've got to get this mess cleaned up before we leave," he said.

"We'll find the horses and get the rest of the supplies loaded," Canyon said.

"Maybe," Fisher said, "I'll even take the time to swear in some new deputies."

"Good deputies are hard to find," Wilmot said and walked away before Fisher could reply.

As O'Grady and Wilmot were walking to retrieve the horses, O'Grady asked, "Are you going to dig at him like that all the way to Texas?"

"I hadn't thought about it," Wilmot said, "but maybe I will." He looked at the big redheaded agent and asked, "Don't you think I have a right?"

"Maybe," Canyon said, "maybe you do, but not while we're depending on each other for our lives. I don't think it would be a good idea. I'm asking you not to do it."

Wilmot hesitated and then said, "All right."

"All right?" Canyon said. "Just like that?"

"Why not?" Wilmot said. "You're doing me a favor by coming along, aren't you? Taking time out from your life to help me straighten out mine? Why shouldn't I do you a favor, too?"

Canyon waited, and when there was nothing further he said, "Thanks, Tom. I appreciate it."

"Sure," Wilmot said. "Now let's go and find those horses."

13

Tom Wilmot was true to his word. During the entire trip to Texas he was civil to Dan Fisher and did not once gibe at the younger man. Canyon spoke to Fisher only when he absolutely had to, but during the trip he found himself liking the man. He appeared to be a hard worker and never slacked off. He was invariably the first one up in the morning and usually had at least coffee and sometimes breakfast ready when they rose. He usually took care of the horses at night, as well.

Canyon found himself watching Wilmot carefully during the trip. As they left Rayford he was still not convinced that Wilmot had the stamina for such a trip. He watched the man closely the first few days, both on the trail and in camp. He seemed naturally weary in the evenings as they camped, but to his credit no more so than himself or Fisher. Initially Canyon figured he was either doing real well, or he was covering up real well. After a few days, though, he gave the man the credit he deserved. He had worked hard around the ranch for three weeks trying to get himself in shape for this trip, and the hard work had paid off.

As for himself, Canyon was wondering just how long he was going to have to put his own life on hold for this. Once they reached the town of Watley—

about twenty miles from Lubbock—it remained to be seen what kind of trail the January brothers would have left to follow. It would certainly have helped if the brothers were known in the town. It would help even more if they *lived* there. The only report Canyon had received was that they were last seen there. He'd much prefer to find out they lived there, or nearby, than they had robbed a bank there.

If they were going to have to track the men from Watley, Canyon wondered just how long his superior, Rufus Wheeler, was going to put up with his absence. That kind of a hunt could take six days, six weeks, or six months. How much time, he wondered, were Wilmot and Fisher willing to put into this? Since the carrot on the end of the stick was sheriff's job in Rayford, neither man could afford to be away from Rayford for any great length of time. If either of them did stay on the trail longer than the other it would be Wilmot. He had more to prove—that he was as good a man with one arm as he was with two—and more to achieve—getting revenge on the men who cost him that arm.

Canyon himself did not figure that he could afford more than two more weeks before he had to get back to his own life, and his own responsibilities.

When they reached Watley, Texas, they were pretty worn out from two weeks on the trail. They looked like they were wearing every mile of dirt on their clothes.

"Let's get the horses taken care of," Canyon said, "and then get some rooms. I'm for a bath."

"I want to talk to the local law," Wilmot said.

"I think we'd make a better impression if we did that after we cleaned up," Canyon said, "don't you, Tom?"

Wilmot looked down at himself, then at the other two men and said, "I guess we do look like saddle tramps."

"Right," Canyon said.

"Let's get to it, then," Fisher said.

"Dan," Wilmot said, "why don't you hand over your horse to Canyon and you can get us some rooms."

"Yeah," O'Grady said, "and you can get to the bathtub first, too."

"Sounds good to me," Fisher said.

They rode to the hotel, where Fisher dismounted and went inside after handing his reins to Canyon.

"Any particular reason you suggested that?" Canyon asked Wilmot as they rode to the livery.

"No," Wilmot said. "I just thought it made sense."

Canyon was glad to hear that. It was evidence that Wilmot was still thinking straight.

When they left the horses at the livery Wilmot's missing arm did not escape the notice of the young man working there. While he took their horses and listened to Canyon's instructions his eyes were pinned to Wilmot's empty sleeve. Canyon watched his friend carefully to see how he would react. He was pleased to see that Wilmot withstood the attention calmly.

They took their saddlebags and rifles, along with Fisher's—which Canyon quite logically carried—and started walking to the hotel. Wilmot had the saddlebags over his right shoulder, and was holding the rifle with his left hand.

"When you gonna stop watching me?" Wilmot asked.

"What do you mean?"

"Come on, Canyon," Wilmot said. "You think I

don't know how close you been watching me the whole trip?"

"I'm just . . . concerned, Tom, that's all."

"You think I'm gonna go crazy on you, don't you? Like in the saloon back in Rayford?"

"Well, you did get us into a heap of trouble with that move, didn't you?"

"I sure did, and I learned my lesson from it, too."

"Well . . . that's good."

"I tell you what, Canyon," Wilmot said, good-naturedly. "You just go on watching me. I don't mind at all. I just know that I'm going to prove to you that I'm completely healed, in body *and* mind."

"Nothing would please me more than to find out that's true, Tom."

"You're a good friend, Canyon," Wilmot said, "probably better than I deserve."

Canyon didn't answer. Unbidden, the sight of Tom Wilmot's wife came to him, with her dress tossed up over her head, and he didn't *feel* like such a good friend.

"If you weren't," Wilmot went on, "you wouldn't be here, would you?"

"I guess not, Tom."

"I mean," Wilmot said, "you're not here for any other reason but to help me. Unlike our friend Sheriff Fisher, that is."

"He's got his own reasons, all right."

"He sure does—to hold onto my job. But that's gonna change. You wait and see."

"I hope you get exactly what you want, Tom."

"Oh, I will, Canyon," Wilmot said, "I will."

The Watley Hotel had only one bathtub, so they took turns. Fisher used it first, followed by O'Grady and then Wilmot. At one point during his bath Canyon's foot slipped and he almost fell while getting out of the tub. This made him wonder if he shouldn't offer some assistance to Wilmot, at least in getting in and out of the tub. He decided not to make the offer for two reasons. Number one, it might embarrass Wilmot, and for a man with something to prove, that might have done too much damage. His second reason was personal. It would have exposed him to Wilmot's naked injury, and he didn't know if he could have trusted himself not to stare. That, too, would have been embarrassing—to both of them.

After they were all bathed and changed—without incident, Canyon was glad to see—they decided to eat first, and wash some dust from their throats, before going to see the local law.

They went to the town's lone saloon and ordered three beers, and then found that they could also get some sandwiches there. It was a simple meal, beer and beef sandwiches, but it was better than anything they had eaten on the trail.

Over dinner they discussed how they would present themselves to the sheriff of Watley.

"I have no jurisdiction," Fisher said, "so it won't do any good to show him my badge."

"Sure it will, Dan," Wilmot said. "It'll establish a bond between you and him, lawman to lawman."

"I wouldn't want him to think I was trying to exert some sort of authority, or influence."

"So you don't," Wilmot said. "You simply tell him that you are the sheriff of Rayford, but that you're not here in any official capacity."

Fisher looked at Canyon, who said, "It sounds like a good idea to me. At least it'll keep us from getting the usual looks strangers in town get from the law."

"Okay," Fisher said, convinced, "so we introduce ourselves. Then what?"

"Then we tell him why we're here," Wilmot said. Canyon decided to let his friend do the explaining. It was, after all, his show.

"The real reason?" Fisher asked.

"Why not?" Wilmot asked. "We're not doing anything illegal."

"After that," Canyon said, "I hope he'll be able to tell us something that will help us." He decided to speak up because it looked to him like Wilmot and Fisher were falling into their old sheriff/deputy relationship. If Fisher had noticed that, it might have caused some tension. A three-way conversation would keep that from happening.

"Well," Fisher said, "I guess we might as well go and do it. If he can't help us, we'll have to get moving again."

"Not before we talk to some other people in town," Wilmot said. "The kind of bad boys the Januarys are, they couldn't have been in town without someone noticing them."

"You're right, of course," Fisher said, and Canyon thought that it cost the man something to admit that. "Well, let's hope they held up a bank, or something. That would get them remembered, wouldn't it?"

"It sure would," Canyon said, just to be part of the conversation again. "Let's go."

14

The sheriff was identified by a sign on a piece of wood hung outside his office. A crude handwriting said his name was Sheriff G. Bates.

"I hope he sheriffs better than he writes," Wilmot said.

"Maybe he didn't write it," Fisher said.

"It doesn't matter," O'Grady said, before the sign became an issue. "Let's go inside."

As they entered it occurred to Canyon that maybe only one of them should have gone, instead of the three of them in force, but it was too late to do anything about it. Besides, that would have just started a discussion about which one.

As they entered, the man seated behind the desk looked up and eyed them speculatively. His suspicion was natural when a lawman was confronted by strangers in his town.

"Can I help you gents?" he asked.

"You Sheriff Bates?" Wilmot asked.

The man took a moment to inspect Wilmot's missing arm none too discreetly and then said, "Yeah, that's me." He was about fifty, gray-haired and overweight.

Wilmont looked at Fisher then, as if to say, "Well, go ahead."

"I'm Sheriff Dan Fisher, from Rayford, Colorado," Fisher said.

"Colorado," Sheriff Bates said, surprised. "You're a little off the beaten path, aren't you?"

"I'm, uh, not here officially," Fisher said.

"Why are you here, then?"

"We're looking for some men."

"Why?" Bates asked.

"Shouldn't your next question be who?" Wilmot asked.

Bates looked at Wilmot and said, "Okay, who are *you*?"

"My name's Tom Wilmot," Wilmot said, "and this is Canyon O'Grady."

"Deputies?" Bates asked.

"No," Canyon said.

"I'm the former sheriff of Rayford, Colorado," Wilmot said.

"The former sheriff," Bates repeated.

"That's right."

"And you're the present sheriff?" he asked Fisher.

"That's right."

Bates looked at O'Grady and asked, "Are you the sheriff of anywhere?"

Canyon didn't like the man's attitude and wished he could have told him, "No, I'm a United States Secret Service agent." Instead he just said, "No."

Bates looked away from him then, as if he was of no importance.

"You got a badge?" Bates asked Fisher.

Fisher took his badge out of his pocket and showed it to the man.

"Actually," Bates said in response, "that don't mean very much. You could have gotten that badge from anywhere."

"Are you saying you don't believe—" Fisher started, but Bates stopped him with a raised hand.

"It don't matter what I believe," Bates said. "Tell me what you fellas want in my town."

"I told you," Fisher said. "We're looking for some men."

"What men?"

"The January brothers," Fisher said. "Carl and Sam. You know them?"

"The Januarys," Bates said, as if he was thinking it over.

"You know who they are," Wilmot said.

Bates looked at the one-armed man and asked, "What makes you say that?"

"You're a lawman," Wilmot said. "There's been paper out on those boys for years. You must have seen it."

"And if I say I ain't?" Bates asked.

"Well," Wilmot said, "that'd make you a liar."

"Tom," Canyon said, warningly.

"That's brave talk for a one-armed man," Bates said, coldly.

"I can back it up," Wilmot said.

"Can you, now?"

"We're getting off on the wrong foot here, gents," Canyon said. "Sheriff, we came here to ask you for your help."

"Your friend here's got a funny way of showing it," Bates said. "Just what is it these January boys did that's got you coming all this way?"

"Them and some friends of theirs robbed a bank in Rayford," Fisher said, "and killed some people."

"When did that happen?" Bates asked.

"About nine months ago," Fisher said.

"Nine months?" Bates said. "That's a long time to

follow a cold trail. That happen while you were sheriff?"

"No," Wilmot said, answering for Fisher, "I was sheriff then."

"Letting them boys rob your bank and kill your citizens lose you your job?" Bates asked.

Canyon watched Wilmot very carefully.

"No," Wilmot said, evenly, "they got me out of the way first by bushwhacking me and shooting off my arm."

"I was deputy then," Fisher said, "but me and the other deputy couldn't stop them."

"Well, why did it take you so long to come after them?" the sheriff of Watley asked.

"It took me a little time to get back on my feet after losing my arm," Wilmot said, frankly.

"You think bringing them back is gonna get you your arm back?"

"My reasons are none of your business, Sheriff."

"I think they are—"

"Sheriff," Canyon said, interrupting the man, "why are you being so difficult about this?"

"Hey," Bates said, "I don't know any of you fellas from Adam. You bust into my office asking me questions—"

"We didn't bust in," Fisher said.

"—claiming you're lawmen, or ex-lawmen," Bates went on. "I don't owe you fellas nothin'."

"Nobody said you did," Canyon said. "We just thought we might get your cooperation in tracking down murderers who are supposed to have been seen in your town."

"Who says they were seen here?" Bates asked. He was looking at Fisher, who had no idea where O'Grady had gotten the information.

"That's our information," was all Canyon would say.

Bates sat behind his desk shaking his head.

"Are you gonna help us or not?" Wilmot asked.

Bates looked at all three of them in turn and said, "I'll have to think about it."

"What's there to think about—" Wilmot started to ask, but Canyon cut him off.

"Okay, Sheriff," he said, "you think about it and we'll come and see you tomorrow."

"Maybe by then you can teach your one-armed friend some manners," Bates said.

Both O'Grady and Fisher stepped in front of Wilmot and got him turned around before he could do anything.

Outside Wilmot pushed them away and said, "He knows them, damn it. He's covering up for them."

"We don't know that," Fisher said.

"We do know that he wasn't real cooperative," Canyon said, "and he kept baiting Tom, for some reason."

"Let's go back inside and make him talk," Wilmot said.

"That's not going to work, Tom," Canyon said. "Let's just give him tonight to think it over and see what he says tomorrow."

"And what do we do until then?" Fisher asked.

"I suggest we start asking some questions," Canyon replied. "If we get the right answers, we might not even need the sheriff."

The three men split up and for the next few hours asked questions around town. They had agreed to meet later in the saloon, and all three showed up bearing the same information.

"They were here, all right," Fisher said as he sat down with O'Grady and Wilmot.

"We know," Canyon said.

"How?"

"They beat up a storekeeper and wrecked his store," Wilmot said.

"That's what I heard," Fisher said.

"This doesn't make sense," Canyon said

"What?" Fisher asked.

"Well, Bates had to know we'd find out about the Januarys from someone else in town. I mean, *everybody* seems to know they were here, so why would he lie? I mean, how could he expect to get away with it?"

"He didn't lie," Wilmot said.

"What?" Fisher said.

"Well, not really," Wilmot said. "He just wasn't very cooperative."

"Well, maybe he'll be more cooperative now that we already know," Fisher said. "Maybe we should go back and ask him where the Januarys are now, because they sure as hell aren't in his jail."

"Why would they be?" Canyon asked. "The incident with the storekeeper took place over a month ago. They could be long gone, by now."

"I don't think so," Wilmot said. "I agree with Dan. I think Bates knows them, and knows where they are. Why else would he try to help them by keeping quiet?"

"Maybe," Canyon said, "he's just afraid of them."

"Then if that's the case," Fisher said, "maybe we just have to make him more afraid of us."

15

They decided to spend the rest of the evening in each other's company, so they remained right there in the saloon. They took a back table and watched the place fill up as it got later and later. A couple of girls started working the floor, and a couple of poker games started up at other tables.

"I think I'll play some poker," Wilmot said at one point.

"Why?" Fisher asked.

Wilmot shrugged and said, "For something to do, I guess. Besides, conversation at this table has become boring." That was because for a good half hour none of them had said anything.

Wilmot finished his beer and walked over to one of the poker tables.

"You fellas mind another hand," he asked, and quickly added, "seein' as how that's all I've got, that is."

The men at the table were stunned for a moment, but as Wilmot laughed they all laughed and invited him to pull up a chair.

"You think that's a good idea?" Fisher asked Canyon.

"Doesn't matter what I think. It's done."

"He thinks he's running the show," Fisher said.

"He is," Canyon said. "I thought you knew that when you signed on."

"I didn't sign on," Fisher said. "I came along. That doesn't mean I have to listen to him. You heard him. Most of the time he's treating me like I'm still his deputy."

"Put up with it," Canyon said. "It's not worth arguing over."

"Maybe you like him telling you what to do," Fisher said. "I don't."

"Then go back to Rayford."

"Sure," Fisher said, "you'd like that—you'd both like that. I go back empty-handed, and then the two of you show up with the Januarys, or some of the others . . . or the *bank's* money."

"Forget about the money. That's a long time gone."

"You're probably right," Fisher said. "I don't understand you, O'Grady."

"What don't you understand, Fisher? I'll try to explain it to you."

While he spoke Canyon was watching the room. He noticed two men standing at the bar. They seemed to have taken an interest in the poker game that Wilmot had joined.

"Why are you doing this?" Fisher asked. "That's what I don't understand. What's in this for you?"

"Nothing."

Fisher waited a moment, then said, "That doesn't explain anything. If there's nothing in it for you, why do it?"

Canyon inclined his head toward Wilmot and said, "Because that man is my friend, and he needs help."

"So you put your own life on hold, for friendship?" Fisher asked.

"Can you think of a better reason?"

"I can't think of *any* reason—"

"Forget that," Canyon said. "We may have trouble."

"Where?"

"Don't turn around. Just do what I say."

Fisher rolled his eyes and said, "Now *you* want to run the show."

"Quiet," Canyon said. "There are two men standing at the bar, about midway. They're dressed in trail clothes, one with a black leather vest. They're pretty interested in watching Tom."

"How long they been watching?"

"Since he sat down, and now two more men walked in, and I'd swear that they know the two at the bar."

"We're being set up."

"I think so," Canyon answered. "Take your mug over to the far end of the bar and get it refilled, then stay there. Keep your eye on the two at the bar. Got it?"

"I understand."

"Okay, so go."

Slowly, Fisher stood up, picked up his empty mug, and walked to the far end of the bar. Since they were sitting in the back, that put him in the front of the room.

Canyon watched as the man got his mug refilled and then stood there sipping it. While he was doing that two other men walked into the place. Canyon was sure he saw a glance pass between them and the two at the bar. They walked to the other poker game, supposedly to watch, but they were actually watching Fisher.

The second pair of men had moved to the side wall and were leaning on it, trying to look uninterested in anything. Canyon knew they were watching him.

The agent knew now that his life depended on just

how recovered Tom Wilmot was from his crippling injury. He was going to have to take care of the third pair of men, the ones watching Fisher, so that Fisher wouldn't get killed. Fisher, on the other hand, was going to have to handle the two at the bar, so that Wilmot didn't get killed. That meant that Wilmot would have to handle the two men who were watching him. If his friend *didn't* notice what was going on, there was a good chance that Canyon was going to end up dead.

And all of this was assuming that there were no other men in the room who were in on the setup.

Canyon figured that the men had to have been sent by Sheriff Bates, but he couldn't dwell on that now. He could feel the tension crackling in the air. He only hoped that Wilmot's senses were not too dull from nonuse for him to notice it, as well.

In a few minutes the room was going to be filled with flying lead. He only hoped that too many innocent bystanders didn't end up getting hurt.

It took a half an hour while the men decided to make their move, which suited Canyon. That just gave Wilmot more time to notice what was going on. Wilmot was winning, however, which indicated that he was concentrating on the game. Maybe it wasn't wise to wait for them to make the first move, but when it was all over it was going to be important that witnesses can say the *other* men made the first move.

When one of the girls came over to the table to ask Canyon if he wanted a beer, he told her to bring one. He had no intention of drinking it, though. He was going to need all his faculties as sharp as they could be. He noticed that Fisher was also nursing the same beer he had ordered half an hour ago.

The saloon continued to fill up, and Canyon decided that's what the men were waiting for. They were probably planning to make their move when the room was very crowded and hope to slip away in the confusion. That also meant that they were liable to try some backshooting.

Suddenly Canyon found himself filled with anger. Not only had a man sent a group of backshooters after them, but that man was also the town sheriff.

He was about to give into his waning patience when the men at the bar pushed away from it, and he knew that it was going to happen now.

He watched the men in the front of the room and they leaned toward Fisher. He dared not sneak a glance at the men who were targeting him. He was going to have to depend on Wilmot for that.

The men who were at the bar started moving toward Wilmot and the poker table, and as they did, they spread apart.

Fisher saw what was happening and knew there were too many men between him and the two would-be assassins. The situation was made even worse because the two men were also putting some distance between themselves.

Fisher knew there was only one thing he could do. He drew his gun and fired the first shot into the ceiling.

Canyon heard the shot and saw most of the men in the place instinctively fall to the floor. The six would-be assassins were still standing and were frozen for just a moment as they tried to decide what had happened. Obviously none of them had fired the shot.

Canyon stood up just as the first two men drew their guns, with intentions of shooting Wilmot. There was no way Fisher could wait. He fired, and all hell broke loose.

Wilmot stood up and drew his gun. He reached for the table to turn it over, but he was reaching with his right hand, and there was no right hand. He fired at the set of men who were targeting Canyon, while Canyon fired across the room at the men who were getting set to fire at Fisher. Fisher, meanwhile, was still firing at the two men who were behind Wilmot.

The assassins, intent on their targets, were caught by surprise when they were fired upon from another direction. They tried to recover, but were caught trying to decide between firing at their targets, or in the direction the shots were coming from. When they finally fired their guns it was into the floor and walls and ceiling while O'Grady's, Fisher's, and Wilmot's shots were smacking solidly into flesh and bone.

The action took only a few seconds to unfold, and when it was over all six assassins were on the floor. A stunned silence hung in the air as patrons of the saloon tried to figure out what the hell had happened.

O'Grady, Fisher, and Wilmot converged in the center of the room.

"You hurt?" Canyon asked both of them.

"I'm fine," Fisher said.

"I had a goddamned full house," Wilmot said.

Since they were unhurt they fanned out and went to check the bodies.

"Dead," Canyon said of his two.

"These, too," Wilmot added.

"Mine, too," Fisher said.

"Anybody else hurt?" Canyon asked, looking around the room.

Slowly men began to stand up, all apparently unhurt, a shocked silence still in the air.

"Jesus . . ." somebody said.

"What happened . . ." another voice asked.

"Somebody get the sheriff!" someone called out.

O'Grady, Fisher, and Wilmot exchanged glances, and then O'Grady said aloud, "That sounds like a pretty good idea to me."

16

When Sheriff Bates entered the saloon O'Grady, Fisher, and Wilmot were lined up against the bar, each with a beer in their hands. It was Canyon's idea. Make sure the lawman sees them as soon as he walks in, and watch his face. When Bates did see them, a few emotions crossed his face. First disbelief, then puzzlement, and finally anger. As he approached them he managed to drive all three from his face. Behind him one deputy trailed, gun in hand.

He looked at the six bodies on the floor, and around at the sparse assemblage of patrons who were still in the place. Many of them had given up and gone home. They didn't want to be around if lead started flying again.

Bates finally looked at the three strangers in town and said, "What the hell happened?"

Canyon said in a low voice, "You really want to talk about this here, Sheriff?"

"What are you talking about?" Bates demanded. He looked past them at the bartender and said, "Ed, what the hell went on here?"

"Damned if I know, Sheriff," the man said. "One minute it's quiet, and the next minute all hell broke loose."

"All hell, huh?" Bates said.

It was obvious to Canyon that the sheriff was confused. He had expected to respond to the shooting and find three dead strangers. He walked now to each of the six dead men, checking them. Canyon was sure he was just stalling for time.

"All right," Bates said, "let's go over to my office and see if we can sort this out."

The sheriff turned to the other people in the room and said, "I need anyone who saw something to come over to my office."

Nobody moved.

Bates turned to the bartender and said, "Ed, I want you at my office."

"But I didn't see nothing, Sheriff."

"I want you anyway," Bates said. He turned to O'Grady, Fisher, and Wilmot and said, "I'll need your guns."

Wilmot was the first to respond. "We'll hold on to our guns, Sheriff."

"Come on," Bates said, speaking in turn to Fisher and Wilmot. "You're a lawman and you're an ex-lawman. You know I need your guns."

Fisher and Wilmot still hesitated, so Canyon drew his gun and held it out to Bates. He doubted that they would be shot down in the street, or in the sheriff's office, and he truly doubted that Bates would do his own shooting. He saw no harm in giving up their guns at this point.

"Damn it," Wilmot said, and held out his gun.

The deputy relieved Fisher of his.

"Let's go," Bates said, "we got some talking to do."

"I've never been in jail before," Fisher said, looking around at the walls of the cell. "I mean, not with the door locked, anyway."

"It's just another room," Wilmot said. "We'll be out soon enough. He can't hold us."

"He can't hold us?" Fisher said. "He tried to have us killed, remember?"

"And he's more likely to let us go so he can have another try at us," Canyon said. "He can't keep us in here without charging us, and I don't think he wants to do that."

"Why not?" Fisher asked.

"He doesn't want us in court telling a judge that the sheriff tried to have us killed, does he?"

"I guess not . . ." Fisher said. He got up and walked to the cell door and tried it again, as if he couldn't believe it was locked.

Bates had walked them back to the office and made a show out of asking them each what had happened. They all told the same story, that they were just passing the time in the saloon when six men came in and drew their guns.

"Ed?" Bates said to the bartender.

"I told you, Sheriff, I didn't see nothin'."

"Who do you think fired the first shot, Ed?" Bates asked.

"Well," the man said, thinking hard, "I think I recall that. I'm pretty sure it was this feller." He pointed at Fisher.

"He fired the first shot?" Bates said, pouncing on the statement.

"The more I think about it, the surer I am, Sheriff," Ed said. "He fired the first shot."

"All right—"

"In the air," the man added.

Bates stopped, stunned, and then said, "What?"

"He fired his gun into the ceiling," the bartender

said. "I remember now. I was wondering why he was doin' that, and *then* all hell broke loose."

"Okay, Ed—"

"Them other fellers drew their guns and then the shootin' started—"

"That's enough, Ed!" Bates said. "You can go."

"Thanks, Sheriff."

The bartender got up and left, and Bates was alone in the room with the three strangers.

"Why'd you do it, Sheriff?" Canyon asked.

"Do what?"

"Try to have us killed," Wilmot said. "It wasn't a smart move."

"I don't know what—"

"We asked around, Sheriff," Canyon said. "You knew we'd do that. You must have known we'd find out that the Januarys were here. I don't understand why'd you lie."

"Or why you'd send guns after us," Fisher said.

"What do those boys have on you?" Canyon asked.

"That's enough," Bates said. He stood up and drew his gun, and for a moment Canyon was afraid he had read the man wrong. He *could* shoot them now and claim that they jumped him. Canyon could see that the others were having the same thoughts.

"Let's go," Bates said.

"Where?" Canyon asked.

"You fellas are gonna spend the night in jail."

"For what?" Wilmot asked.

"I'll think of something."

"You can't do that," Fisher said.

Bates showed Fisher a tight grin and said, "Just watch me."

* * *

The morning sunlight sifting between the bars woke Canyon the next morning.

"You sleep late," Wilmot said.

Canyon looked over at the other bunk and saw Wilmot already sitting up. He and the one-armed man were sharing a cell, while Fisher had a cell all to himself. In the other cell the sheriff of Rayford was still asleep.

"Wanna wake him?" Wilmot asked.

"What for?" Canyon said. "Let him sleep."

"Well," Wilmot said, "as far as I'm concerned we found the January boys."

"How do you figure that?"

"The sheriff's got to know them," Wilmot said, "and he's got to know where they are, otherwise why's he tryin' to help them?"

"Maybe he's afraid of them," Canyon said.

"Maybe," Wilmot said, "but I'd rather believe that he's friendly with them, and coverin' up for them."

"That's no way to keep his job."

"Maybe he's not worried about keeping his job."

"Maybe not."

After a moment of silence, during which Canyon stretched, trying to work out the kinks, Wilmot asked, "Think he'll shoot us trying to escape?"

"He would have done it last night, when it was dark," Canyon said.

"So he's gonna let us go?"

"He has to."

"Yeah," Wilmot said, "that's what I figure, too."

"When?" Fisher's voice asked from the next cell.

"When what?"

"When will he let us out?" Fisher sat up and rubbed his face.

"Soon," Canyon said, "he'll let us out soon."

At that point the door to the office opened and Bates appeared, jingling his keys.

"Time for you to go and buy your own breakfast," Bates said. "I ain't feedin' you today."

He opened Canyon's and Wilmot's cell first, and then Fisher's. They followed the lawman back into his office, where he gave them back their guns.

"Figured out it wasn't our fault, huh?" Canyon asked.

"Yeah," Bates said, "you fellas are as innocent as snow, right?"

"You want to tell us now about the January boys?" Wilmot asked.

"January?" Bates said, thoughtfully. He pointed at Wilmot and said, "Now ain't that a month? The first one, ain't it?"

"Look, you—"

"Come on, Tom," Canyon said. "Let's get cleaned up, and get some breakfast."

Outside Wilmot stopped and said, "We can't let him get away with this."

"He won't get away with it," Canyon replied.

"You got a plan?" Fisher asked.

"We're all going to come up with a plan."

"Oh yeah?" Wilmot asked. "When?"

"Right after breakfast."

17

They got cleaned up and had breakfast at a small cafe that was off the main street. Canyon didn't think Bates would send anyone after them this soon after the first try, but they were still better off staying out of sight.

After breakfast they ordered another pot of coffee, because they hadn't come up with a plan yet.

"We've got to remember that we're dealing with a lawman," Fisher said. "He's the law, damn it."

"He's crooked, Dan," Wilmot said. "You know what I always said about crooked lawmen."

"Yeah, yeah, I know," Fisher said, "it just goes against the grain to go up against a man wearing a badge."

"Well," Canyon said, "that's what we're going to have to do. We're going to have to go up against him."

"I'm not going to kill another lawman," Fisher said.

"Don't worry," Wilmot said, giving Canyon a look, "we ain't gonna kill him. What are we gonna do to him, Canyon?"

"We're going to talk to him, Tom, just talk to him."

"All we got to do is figure out when," Wilmot said. "Tonight?"

"We'd have to stay alive that long," Canyon said.

"I don't want to spend the whole day looking over my shoulder."

"When, then?" Fisher asked.

"Why not now?" Canyon said. "Now sounds like a good time, to me."

"What about following him?" Fisher asked.

"We could do that," Canyon said, "but there's a chance that he'll never go near the Januarys again. No, I think we're going to have to get him to tell us what he knows."

"I agree."

"Fisher?"

The sheriff of Rayford hesitated and then said, "All right, but I'll say again, I won't be a party to killing him."

"If we kill him," Canyon said, "he can't tell us a thing."

Bates had to come out of his office sometime, and when he did they were there, watching. Wilmot and Fisher had taken up positions up and down the street, while Canyon settled into a doorway across from the jail. As it turned out they did intend to follow him, but only until they found a good place to waylay him. Of course, they couldn't all follow him without being seen, so it was decided that O'Grady would be the primary shadow, while the others would stay well ahead and well behind, available to help if help was needed, but not so close that they would be seen.

Bates appeared to be making his rounds. He sauntered along the town streets at an easy pace. Canyon noticed that very few people greeted their sheriff, leading him to believe that the man was not that popular. He wondered how many times the man had been reelected, and if he would be reelected again.

They followed him for half a day without coming

upon an opportunity to act. While Canyon kept his eyes on Bates, it was the job of Wilmot and Fisher to keep their eyes out for another attempt on their lives. They agreed that an attempt would probably not be made on any one of them separately. When it came it would be against them as a group. Killing one of them would not accomplish anything.

While following the sheriff Canyon started to wonder if anyone coming to town asking about the Januarys would be killed, or if it was just them. If it was them, that would mean that the Januarys knew they were coming, and how could *that* be? After better than nine months they certainly wouldn't be expecting anyone from Rayford.

At about three o'clock Bates stopped into the telegraph office and stayed for a few minutes, then left. Canyon was able to see through the window that the man was indeed sending a telegram. To the Januarys? he wondered. Was this the first such telegram sent, or the second? Perhaps he had already sent one the day before for instructions, and this one was to report failure and ask for further instructions. Canyon reminded himself to ask Wilmot more questions about the Januarys. For one thing, he wanted to know how smart they were. Was the Rayford job theirs, or were they following someone?

When dusk arrived Bates was back in his office. O'Grady waved at Fisher and walked to join Wilmot. Moments later Fisher was there, as well.

"Well, that accomplished a lot," Fisher said. "What do we do now?"

"We skipped lunch," Wilmot said. "I suggest we have dinner and discuss it further."

"All right," Canyon said, even though he thought

he already knew what their next move should be. "Let's go and eat."

Over dinner Canyon said, "We've got to push this."

"You're in a hurry?" Fisher said. "Want to get back to your life?"

"I want us all to be able to get on with our lives; that's why I want to press the issue before they try for us again and succeed."

"He has a point," Wilmot said around a mouthful of vegetables. O'Grady and Fisher had ordered steaks. Rather than have to ask one of them to cut his meat for him, Wilmot had ordered a plate of vegetables.

"All right, so how do we push it?" Fisher asked.

"That's easy," Canyon said. "We just go in and get him."

"Suits me," Wilmot said.

"Uh, hold on," Fisher said, nervously. "What do we mean by 'go in and get him'?"

"The boy's showing nerves again," Wilmot said. "Maybe you should go home, Dan."

It was the first time since they had left Rayford that Wilmot had prodded Fisher.

"Look," Fisher said, "I'm just naturally concerned about going up against the law—"

"Look," Canyon said, "this lawman you're so concerned about sent six men to kill us."

"We don't know that," Fisher said.

"*We* know that," Wilmot said, indicating Canyon and himself.

"We're going into his office tonight and we're going to ask him," Canyon said. "We're going to confront him and make him tell us what he knows about Carl and Sam January's whereabouts."

"All right," Fisher said, after a moment, "all right, I'll go with you, but on the condition—"

"No," Canyon said, "no conditions. If you're not ready to go with us and do what has to be done, then maybe you should go back home."

They finished their meal in strained silence after that, and when they were ready to leave O'Grady said to Fisher, "Well? What's it going to be?"

Fisher threw his napkin down on the table and said, "When do we do it?"

"Tonight," Canyon said, "when it's nice and dark."

"What do we do until then?"

"We stay out of sight," Canyon replied, "and we stay alive."

In his office Gordon Bates sat behind his desk, eating his dinner which he had brought in from the cafe—the same cafe where O'Grady, Wilmot, and Fisher had eaten their dinner. He ate without much appetite. He was still disgusted with himself for setting the three men up to be killed, and disgusted with the six men who had gotten killed, instead. In fact, he was disgusted with the whole matter. If he wasn't so afraid of Carl and Sam January, and the men they rode with, he'd give up his badge and go live someplace on a farm, by himself. If he did that, though, he knew they'd find him.

He had to come up with somebody who could do the job. He knew if he failed again the January brothers would come and do the job themselves, and when they finished with it, they'd take care of him, too, and very possibly the whole town.

That was it. He'd just convince himself that what he was doing he was doing for the whole town—but that didn't make his dinner taste any better, either.

* * *

Sam and Carl January stood in front of Lou Boudreau, who had summoned them into his cabin. "What's this I hear about some lawmen from Colorado asking questions about you in Watley?"

Sam and Carl exchanged nervous glances. As vicious as they were, when it came to Lou Boudreau they were downright afraid of the man. They were bigger than he was, and stronger, but he was smarter, and brains scared the hell out of the January brothers.

"Well?" Boudreau said.

"We're taking care of it," Sam said, "ain't we Carl?"

"That's right."

"Where exactly are these lawmen from?" Boudreau asked.

"Rayford, Colorado."

Boudreau frowned. He was forty-four, six foot and thin as a rail, with thick black hair that came to a widow's peak. His eyebrows were heavy and black, and when he frowned they came together to form one.

"What did we . . . did we pull a job there?"

"Yeah," Carl said. "Eight or nine months back. We hit their bank."

"They're after you for that? After all these months? How did they get onto you?"

"We told you the law there knew us," Sam said.

"We took care of him, didn't we?" Boudreau asked.

"We thought so," Sam said. "We put five bullets into him."

"And he didn't die?" Boudreau asked.

"I guess not," Sam said.

"One of the men looking for us has one arm," Carl said. "That must be him."

"Who knows you in Watley?"

"The sheriff," Sam said. "He rode with us once or twice, before he became a lawman."

"You got control of him?"

"Yeah," Sam said, "that's why we said we're taking care of it."

"You better be," Boudreau said. "If those lawmen find their way here, I ain't gonna like it. Understand?"

"We understand, boss."

"Get out, now."

Sam and Carl left the cabin and went outside, where the other two members of their gang, Dolph Peters and Brad Dawson, were waiting.

"What's goin' on?" Peters asked.

"A job we pulled nine months ago is comin' back on us," Sam said.

"Where were we nine months ago?"

"Colorado," Carl said.

"I don't remember that," Dawson said.

"We put five bullets into the local sheriff."

"I remember *that*," Dawson said. "We fixed him good."

"Not good enough," Sam said. "He's in Watley with two other men, asking about me and Carl."

"Really?" Dawson said. "You and Carl, huh?"

"We're doin' somethin' about it," Sam said.

"You better," Dawson said. "You bring them down on us, Boudreau won't like it."

"Take care of your business, boys," Peters said, and he and Dawson walked away.

Sam January turned to Carl January and said, "You notice how everybody forgets they was with us in Rayford?"

"Yeah," Sam said. "Our friends."

* * *

"Maybe I should go and talk to that storekeeper again," Canyon said.

"Which storekeeper?" Fisher asked.

"The one the Januarys pistol-whipped," Canyon said. "Maybe they said something in front of him."

"We'll come along," Wilmot said.

"I think you fellas should stay here," Canyon said. They were in the saloon, seated at a back table again. It was agreed that there would be no poker tonight, that they would all sit together at the same table. From where they were they could see the entire room, and the front and back doors.

When they had first entered the saloon Ed, the bartender, asked them nervously, "There ain't gonna be no trouble tonight, is there?"

"If there is," Canyon had promised, "it won't be started by us."

Ed seemed to take that as small compensation.

Now Canyon said to Wilmot, "I'll make a smaller target than the three of us walking down the street."

Wilmot shook his head.

"We stick together, Canyon," he said. "Where you go, we go."

Canyon opened his mouth to argue, but then decided that Wilmot was right.

"Okay," he said, "let's go and see what he has to say."

18

After the January brothers left the cabin Lou Boudreau got up and walked to the door to the cabin's second room. He entered and looked at the woman on the bed. She had a sheet thrown over her, but he knew she was naked beneath it. He knew it because he was the one who had taken her clothes from her.

He closed the door behind him and approached the bed. She opened her eyes and looked up at him.

"It's that time again," he said.

The woman sighed and with one hand tossed the sheet aside. He caught his breath, as he did each time he saw her naked. She was a tall woman, five foot ten. She had wide shoulders which nicely accommodated her very large breasts. For such a tall woman she had a slender waist, which made her wide hips look even wider, and her broad buttocks even broader. She had powerful legs and thighs from working on the farm.

As he undressed he studied her and felt his groin tightening. By the time he was naked his erection was huge. He put his hands on her and she closed her eyes as his coarse fingers and palms roamed over her pink nipples, her belly, and her hips. He ended his journey with the fingers of one hand nestled in the wet bush between her legs.

Her name was Paula Burke, and she had been there for about three weeks. For that entire three weeks she had been naked.

Boudreau and his men had stopped at the farm owned by her and her husband, supposedly to water their horses. When Boudreau saw her, though, he knew he had to have her. After they had watered their animals Boudreau had the Januarys pistol-whip her husband. They then lifted her up onto the back of Boudreau's horse. She fought them until Boudreau said he would kill her husband if she didn't go with him. When she asked if he was going to bring her back, he said, "Maybe."

Boudreau figured to cut her loose or kill her when he grew tired of her. The only problem was that he still wasn't tired of her, and was showing no sign of tiring of her.

Boudreau had had a lot of women over the years, some willing and some not so willing. The first time he had taken Paula Burke he had felt her react beneath him. As unwilling as she had been to have sex with him, just moments after he entered her she had been bucking and writhing beneath him like a wild animal, raking his back with her nails, tightening her powerful thighs around his waist and crying out.

After that first time Paula had cried for a long time. She was ashamed because as soon as Boudreau had entered her she had climaxed, something she had done very seldom during her twelve-year marriage to her husband. She had long ago decided that sex was not a big part of her life. Her husband loved her, and was a hard worker and a good provider. When they had sex he enjoyed it very much, and she *pretended* to enjoy it. It was humiliating to think that a brute like

Boudreau could take her to heights she never knew with the man she loved.

The first chance she got she was going to kill Boudreau, and then herself.

She had been waiting three weeks for that chance to come.

When they reached the shopkeeper's store he was very near to closing. He recognized Fisher as they entered, as it had been he whom the man had spoken to the first time.

Canyon could see the scars on the man's face from the pistol-whipping. They were still fresh. Some of them would fade with time, some would not.

Standing next to the man behind the counter was a lovely young woman of about twenty-two or -three. She stiffened when the three men walked into the store and moved closer to the man. Canyon sensed that there was something more between them than just employer and employee. She was either the man's daughter, or a very young wife.

Fisher had told him that the man's name was Collins.

"Hello, Mr. Collins," Fisher greeted.

Collins said to the woman, "This is the sheriff from Colorado I told you about, Mandy. This is my daughter, Mandy."

Mandy Collins visibly relaxed, but remained close to her father. All three men removed their hats, respectfully.

"These are my friends, Mr. Collins," Fisher said, "Canyon O'Grady and Tom Wilmot."

"Mr. Collins," Canyon said.

Mandy Collins's eyes widened when she saw Wilmot's empty sleeve.

"What can I do for you gents?" Collins asked. He was a barrel-chested man in his fifties with gray and black hair that was very coarse and short cropped. He had worked-hardened hands and thick forearms. He would not have submitted to the Januarys easily, Canyon surmised.

"We'd like to ask you a few more questions about what happened to you, Mr. Collins."

"What more can he tell you?" Mandy Collins asked. She had chosen to give her attention to Canyon. "Those animals came in here and pistol-whipped him."

"We understand that, Miss Collins," Canyon said. "We're hoping that they might have said something that will help us find them."

"Like what?" she asked.

"We don't know. Where they were going when they left here, where they had come from."

"I'm sorry," Collins said. "When they came in they started mishandling the merchandise. I called them on it, and they beat me down with their pistols. That's all there is to it." In memory of the incident he reached up and touched his face in several places that were scarred.

"Were you here during the incident, Miss Collins?" Canyon asked.

"I was not," she said. "If I had been I would have gotten a gun and killed them."

Collins put his hand over his daughter's and said, "You would have been killed. I'm glad you were out making deliveries."

"Your father's right, miss," Wilmot said. "They would have killed you without a thought."

"Did they—" she started, then stopped, then

started again. "I'm sorry . . . did they do that to you?"

"Yes, ma'am," he said. "They bushwhacked me and put five bullets into me."

"Oh, my," she said, putting her hand to her mouth.

"Well, thanks for talking to us again, Mr. Collins," Canyon said. "We won't bother you anymore."

"I hope you find them," Collins said.

"I hope you *kill* them," Mandy Collins said.

"Don't worry," Wilmot said to her, "we will."

They left the store and put their hats back on.

"Pretty girl," Wilmot said. "I'm glad she wasn't there."

"Me, too," Canyon said.

"What now?" Fisher asked.

"Now we go back to the saloon," Canyon replied. "It should be dark enough soon for what we have to do."

They were back in the saloon a half an hour when Mandy Collins suddenly appeared at the bat-wing front doors. She stepped inside and started searching the room.

"I'll be right back," Canyon said when he saw her.

"How do you know she's not just looking for her sweetheart?" Wilmot asked.

Canyon grinned and said, "So that's what I'll find out."

He negotiated the crowded room and when she spotted him she smiled and waved at him once, making it obvious that she was indeed looking for him.

"Are you looking for someone in particular, Miss Collins?" he asked as he reached her.

She was wearing the same simple print dress she

had been wearing at her father's store, but she had a shawl around her shoulders.

"I was looking for you," she said, "and I wish you would call me Mandy, Mr. O'Grady."

"All right," he said, "if you'll call me Canyon."

"Canyon," she said, in such a way as to indicate that she was tasting his name. "I like that."

"Yes," he said, "thank you, so do I. Why don't we talk outside. You really don't belong in here."

Outside she said, "Why don't I belong in there?"

"You're too nice, and much too pretty," he said.

She blushed and said, "Thank you."

"What was it you wanted to talk to me about?"

"Something very unpleasant, I'm afraid," she said, pulling the shawl tighter around her shoulders. "I know a woman named Paula Burke. She and her husband have a farm about twenty miles south of town. They come here to buy their supplies."

"Yes," he prompted when she paused.

"Well, they would only come to town every three or four weeks," she said. "The last time Mr. Burke came to town it was to see the doctor, and the sheriff."

"About what?"

"Some men came to their farm, pistol-whipped Mr. Burke and took Paula away with them."

"And he reported it to the sheriff?"

"Yes," she said, "for all the good it did him."

"Has his wife returned?"

"I don't know," she said. "He was here about three weeks ago."

"Around the same time your father was injured?"

"Yes."

"Did Mr. Burke come to town before or after your father was hurt?"

"After," she said.

"So it's possible that the same men stopped at his farm after they left here, on their way to . . . where?"

"I don't know," she said, even though he wasn't actually asking her, but himself.

"That's something for us to find out."

"Then this helps you?" she asked, hopefully.

"It helps a great deal, Mandy," he said. "It gives us a whole other way to go."

"Good," she said. "I want you to find them."

"We will," he said. "Thank you for your help."

"I wish I could do more."

"You've done fine."

There was an awkward moment and then she said, "So, that means you'll be leaving soon?"

"We'll ride out to the Burke farm tomorrow. We'll have to see where we can go from there."

"Will you come back here . . . I mean, I'd like to know if Paula is safe, or not."

"I promise I'll come back and let you know," he said.

"Oh, good," she said, and then lest she sound too eager added, "I mean, I'm very worried about Paula."

"You're a good friend, Mandy."

She blushed again, then said, "Can I ask you a question?"

"Of course."

"What harm have these men done to you?"

"None to me personally," he said.

"Then why have you come all this way looking for them?" she asked.

"Tom Wilmot is a friend of mine, and I want to help him," he explained.

"The man with one arm?"

"That's right. He was the sheriff of his town, and

these men came to town and took that away from him. They also robbed the bank and killed some innocent men. It's important for Tom to prove that he's still capable of doing his job."

"Then that makes you a very good friend, as well," she said.

He smiled and said, "It's not a bad thing to be, is it?"

"No," she said. "I like being a friend . . . and I like making new friends." This last she added almost shyly.

"So do I, Mandy," Canyon said, "so do I."

After Lou Boudreau was finished with Paula Burke he went outside to summon Carl and Sam January again.

"Now what's he want?" Carl said to Sam.

"Maybe he's tired of the woman and wants to give her to us," Sam suggested.

"Ha," Carl said, "not much chance of that, is there?"

When they entered the cabin Boudreau was standing by the fireplace, lighting a cigar. He made them wait until he had it going just right before acknowledging their presence.

"I've decided that you shouldn't leave your fate in the hands of others."

"Huh?" Carl said.

"Go to Watley and take care of this thing yourself," Boudreau said, impatiently.

"How?" Sam asked.

"I don't know how," Boudreau said. "Kill anyone who knows where you are, or kill the three men from Colorado. Just make sure that nobody finds us here. Understand?"

"Sure, Boss," Sam said, "we understand."

"I'm planning our next job and I don't want anything to interfere with it." He pointed the lit end of the cigar at them and said, "Fix it."

19

When it was dark enough O'Grady, Fisher, and Wilmot left the saloon and walked down to the sheriff's office. First Canyon looked in the window to make sure that Bates was there and alone. When he had ascertained that he was, he went back to Fisher and Wilmot.

"Fisher, Tom and I will go in the front door, you cover the back."

"You think he's gonna try to get out the back?"

"Once we're inside we'll let you in," Canyon said.

"Oh, okay."

"After that you'll have to stand by the front window and watch for his deputy—or deputies. We don't know how many he has."

"We've seen only one," Wilmot said. "In a town this size, that might be enough."

"Well, as long as we can't be sure somebody will have to play lookout."

"Why me?" Fisher asked, almost petulant about it.

"We don't have time for this, Fisher," Canyon said, evenly.

Fisher relented and said, "All right," but he wasn't happy. Obviously he still felt he was being treated as the deputy.

"We'll wait five minutes while you get into position," Canyon told him.

The younger man nodded and left them, heading for the nearest alley.

"How do we play it?" Wilmot asked.

"I'll be the calm one," Canyon said, "you be the crazy one. He'll believe that because of your arm."

"Right," Wilmot said. "I'll play it up."

When the five minutes were over they went to the front door and let themselves in, moving quickly. Bates had no chance to react before he was looking down the barrels of their guns.

"Are you crazy?" he demanded.

"Yeah," Wilmot said, "I am."

"I'm the *law* here," Bates said.

"A pretty poor excuse for law, I'd say," Canyon said.

"You can't do this."

"Oh no?" Canyon said. "Watch us. Keep an eye on him," he told Wilmot.

Canyon went to the back door and opened it, admitting Fisher. When they both reentered the office Fisher went directly to the front window.

O'Grady moved around to the front of the desk and holstered his gun. Wilmot still had his out.

"I'll take that," Canyon said, leaning over the desk and taking Bates's gun from his holster.

"You can't get away with this," Bates said. "I'll have you behind bars for this."

Wilmot laughed, and even to O'Grady it sounded like the cackle of a demented man.

"What makes you think you're gonna live long enough to put us behind bars?" he said.

"Hey, Tom," Canyon said, playing the part, "we said we weren't going to kill him."

"You said *you* weren't going to kill him," Wilmot said. "I never said any such thing."

"Hey, wait a minute—" Fisher protested. He wasn't in on the act, so his reactions were going to be real.

"Shut up, Fisher," Wilmot snapped. "Just keep looking out the window."

"What's goin' on here?" Bates demanded. He was starting to look worried. Not frightened yet, but worried.

"I'll tell you what's going on," Canyon said. "You're going to tell us where to find your friends, Carl and Sam January."

"What? I don't know where they are. They're not my friends."

"Hey," Wilmot said, "that's two lies in the same breath. The next time you do that I'm gonna put a bullet in you."

"You're crazy!"

"Stop saying that," Canyon said quickly. "He doesn't like it."

"No, it's okay," Wilmot said, leaning over the desk so he could wave the barrel of the gun right in Bates's face. He did it slowly, describing figure eights in the air.

"He's right, I am crazy," Wilmot continued. "I'll do anything to catch up to those Januarys. See what they did to me?" he asked, pushing his empty sleeve into prominence with a move of his shoulders. "Do you think I would let them get away with this?"

"B-but . . . I didn't have anything to do with it," Bates said.

"You know where they are," Wilmot said. "You've already tried to have us killed to protect them."

"No, you don't understand," Bates said. "I was tryin' to protect the whole *town*."

"Oh sure," Canyon said, "like a good lawman, right? No lawman resorts to murder, Bates."

"Look," Bates said, "I'm tellin' ya, they'll kill me and burn the town to the ground."

In the silence that followed his statement the sound of Wilmot cocking the hammer on his gun was obscenely loud—so loud, in fact, that Bates jumped and Fisher reacted.

"But O'Grady," Fisher said, "you can't let him kill him!"

"I can't control him, Fisher," O'Grady said. "He's out of control."

"Jesus . . ." Bates said. His face was slick with sweat and O'Grady could smell the sickly scent of his fear.

"The way I see it, *Sheriff*," Wilmot said, "you got two choices. You can tell us where to find them so we can keep them from ever coming to town again, or I'll kill you right now." He stopped moving the cocked weapon and pressed it right against Bates's forehead, between his eyes. "What's it gonna be?"

Bates opened his mouth to speak, but he was too dry. He tried to moisten his lips with his tongue a few times before attempting to speak again.

"Okay," he finally said, his voice sounding like a croak, "okay, I'll take you to them."

"Tell us where they are," Canyon said.

"I can't," the frightened man said, and now his voice was a squeak. He cleared his throat and said, "It's too hard. You'll never find them. I'll have to take you there."

Wilmot pressed the gun harder against the man's head and said, "Listen to me good, Bates. Your badge means nothing to me. I'd just as soon kill you as look at you. If you're lying—"

"I'm not lying, I'm not," Bates said, almost blubbering now.

"Good," Wilmot said. He removed the gun and leaned back. The barrel left a small round circle imbedded in the flesh of Bates's head.

"We'll leave at first light, then," Canyon said. "Someone will have to stay with him all night."

"I'll stay," Fisher said.

"No," Wilmot said, "I'll stay with our friend Sheriff Bates. Maybe he'll think he has a chance to jump a one-armed man—a *crazy* one-armed man."

"All right," Canyon said, "you stay with him. We'll pick you up in the morning with the horses."

"You can't leave the man here with *him*," Fisher yelled, pointing at Wilmot. "He'll kill him!"

"Maybe he will," Canyon said. "That'll be up to Sheriff Bates."

Canyon walked to the door and said to Wilmot, "Have a nice night."

"Oh, we will," Wilmot said. "We'll talk about our different approaches to upholdin' the law. Won't we, Sheriff."

Bates nodded jerkily.

"Let's go, Fisher."

"You can't—"

"Let's *go*!" Canyon said, grabbing the man's arm and literally pulling him out the door.

"You said yourself he's out of control," Fisher argued outside.

"It was an act, Fisher," Canyon said.

"An act?"

"That's right. Even you bought into it, so it sure convinced Bates."

"An act," Fisher said, again. "He's not crazy?"

"Well, he might be crazy," Canyon said, with a shrug, "but he's not *that* crazy."

After O'Grady and Fisher left, Wilmot walked to the front door and locked it, then marched Bates into the back so he could lock the back door.

"You can't stay awake all night," Bates said to him. "You got to sleep sometime."

"Ah, you *are* figurin' on jumpin' the one-armed man, aren't you?"

"No, no, I didn't mean that," Bates said, "but my deputy might come along."

"How many deputies you got, Bates?"

"Just the one."

"You better not be lyin' to me," Wilmot said. He was enjoying playing the crazy man—maybe even enjoying it too much.

"No, I swear," Bates said, "just one deputy."

"Well, you better hope he's as good a deputy as you are a sheriff, because if he shows up around here tonight he just might get you killed."

"He won't come," Bates said.

"How do you know?"

"He's never around at night. He's always goofin' off someplace. He's probably at the whorehouse."

"And if he does come around and finds the door locked?" Wilmot asked.

"He'll just go away."

"Sounds to me like you got a deputy you deserve," Wilmot said.

"W-what are we gonna do now?" Bates asked.

"Like you said, we got to get some sleep. Get in the cell."

"What?"

"Into this cell," Wilmot said, pointing to the nearest of the two cells.

Bates got into the cell and Wilmot closed the door, but didn't lock it.

"Make a break for it and I'll kill you," he said.

Wilmot went into the other cell and started searching it.

"What are you lookin' for?" Bates asked.

Once, many years ago, he had been locked in his own jail. Ever since that time he had always kept a key hidden in all of his cells, so that it could never happen again. To his satisfaction, Bates did not turn out to be smart enough to have done that.

"Okay," Wilmot said, "out of that cell and into this one."

"W-what are you doin'?" Bates asked, moving from one cell to the other.

"Just makin' sure you don't get away, Sheriff, that's all. Now get some sleep."

He took the cell keys off a hook on the wall and locked Bates into his own cell. He took the keys with him into the other cell and moved the bunk directly underneath the small, barred window. It would be very difficult for anyone to get a shot off at him at that angle, and he was far enough from the other cell that Bates could not possibly reach him.

"Go to sleep, Bates," Wilmot said. "We've got a big day tomorrow."

He lay there for a while and was almost asleep when Bates spoke up.

"Hey, you asleep?"

"No."

"What're you gonna do with me after tomorrow?" Bates asked. "I mean, after I show you where the January boys are?"

"Gee, I don't know, Bates," Wilmot said. "Me and my partners didn't talk about that, yet. I guess that'll depend on how cooperative you really are."

"I'll cooperate."

"I know you will."

After a few moments of silence Bates said, "They're not gonna be alone out there, you know."

"Bates," Wilmot said, "I'm countin' on it."

20

O'Grady and Fisher spent two hours in the saloon nursing beers before they decided to turn in.

"Should we check on Tom?" Fisher asked as they left the saloon.

"Tom's a big boy, Fisher," Canyon said. "Besides, checking on him would do him more harm than good."

"I'm not worried about that, O'Grady," Fisher said. "My concern is catching the men who robbed the Rayford bank."

"That's funny," O'Grady said.

"What's funny?"

"You weren't concerned with that until you found out that Tom and I were going after them," Canyon said. "You're just worried about being made to look bad by a one-armed man."

"Look," Fisher said, "is it so bad that I'd like to hang onto my job?"

"Fisher," Canyon said, "do you really think a one-armed man has the chance to be elected sheriff, no matter who he is?"

"Tom was a very popular sheriff," Fisher said, sullenly.

"Let me ask you something," Canyon said.

"What?"

"Why couldn't you just bide your time and learn from Tom while you were doing it? What was the rush that you had to take Tom's job while he was laid up?"

"*Somebody* had to do the job," Fisher said, defensively.

"You were already first deputy," Canyon said. "You could have done the job that way until Tom decided whether he still wanted the job or not. If he didn't, I'm sure he would have recommended you for it. Instead, you had to show your disrespect and a lack of loyalty for Tom."

"Abe Gorman offered me the job."

"Right," Canyon said. "He was afraid he'd look bad if his town had a one-armed sheriff. All you had to do was back Tom."

"They would have hired someone else," Fisher said as they reached the hotel.

"Maybe," Canyon said, "maybe they would have hired someone else."

They went inside and up to their rooms without speaking to each other again. Canyon wondered if anything he had said had gotten through to the younger man.

Canyon was in his room about an hour when there was a knock on the door. It was a soft knock, tentative even, which led him to believe that it wasn't Fisher. He did not get the sense that there was any danger, but he took his gun to the door with him anyway. When he opened it, Mandy Collins looked first at his naked torso, and then at the gun in his hand.

"I don't think you're going to need that," she said.

"Sorry," he said, putting the gun behind his back. "You can't be too careful in a strange town."

"Did you think it was . . . one of them?" she asked.

"As I said, I was just being careful. Would you like to come in?"

"Please."

She entered the room and he closed the door. The lamp on his table was on a low flame, and as he went to make it higher she said, "You can leave it low. I'm actually pretty embarrassed about this."

"About what?" he asked, putting his gun back in the holster that was hanging on the bed post.

"About coming here like this, to a man's room, late at night," she said. She was still wearing the same dress and shawl, and she pulled the shawl tightly around her shoulders, as if she was cold. "It's a scandalous thing to do," she said with her back to him.

"Only if you have something scandalous in mind," he said softly.

She turned around now and looked at him.

"I do," she said.

He walked to her and took hold of her shoulders. He'd been with enough women to be reasonably sure he was reading her signals right. He pulled her to him and kissed her. Her mouth softened beneath his and she moaned as he ran his tongue over her teeth. She parted her teeth then and accepted his tongue into her mouth, where it intertwined with hers.

When he broke the kiss she whispered, "Oh, God," with her eyes closed. He could feel her body quivering, and knew it was not because she was nervous.

He removed the shawl and tossed it aside, then undid the buttons on her high-necked dress. He pushed the dress down off her shoulders and leaned over to run his mouth over her smooth skin. He pushed the dress lower, until it was around her waist. Her breasts were a pleasant surprise, fuller than he might have thought seeing her dressed. He cupped them in his hands, lifted them to his mouth so he could suckle the dark brown nipples. She groaned aloud this time and leaned into him.

"Canyon . . ." she said, whispering his name with something akin to reverence, "Oh, Canyon . . . please . . . please . . ."

That was all she said, but he knew what she was asking him.

He removed the remainder of her clothes slowly, running his hands over her buttocks, her thighs, her legs while he was doing it. When she was naked he stepped back and removed his own clothes while she watched. The moan that escaped her lips when she saw his rigid cock was almost anguished. She reached for him, holding him in both hands lightly, and he pushed her back toward the bed while still in her grasp.

When the backs of her knees struck the bed she sat down, still holding him. He ran his hands over her shoulders and her breasts, thumbing the turgid nipples. She bit her lips and pulled on him more insistently.

He got down on his knees then, breaking her hold on him, and began to pepper her thighs with loving kisses. He ran his lips and tongue over the tops of her thighs, and then moved to the soft insides. She spread her legs to accommodate him and then, as if all of her strength had drained out of her, she fell back on the bed, her thighs spread wide.

He explored the soft inner skin of her thighs, nipping it, licking it, working his way up to her dark pubic bush. He took the coarse hair in his mouth, wetting it, and the first time his tongue touched her, and probed her, she shuddered and writhed beneath him, pleasure flowing through her like waves . . . and it was just the beginning . . .

"God . . ." she said later. "That was wonderful."

"Still feel embarrassed?" he asked.

"The truth?"

"Yes."

"Yes, I do," she said. "I've never come to a man's room before, not to . . . to . . . well, not ever!"

"I'm flattered that you picked me."

"I think we picked each other," she said. She slid her hand over his chest, rubbing his nipples with her middle finger. "As soon as you walked into the store. Don't you think?"

"Yes," he said, "I do think so."

"And you'll be leaving soon."

"Yes."

She sighed and slid her hand down over his belly.

"It's a shame," she said.

"That's life, Mandy," he said. "Right person, wrong time, wrong place."

"You sound like you've been through it before."

He smiled and said, "Once or twice, maybe."

"Will you remember me?" she asked.

"Oh yes," he said, "I'll remember you."

She had his penis in her hand now and it was swelling, suffusing with blood.

"Let's make sure of that, okay?" she said.

"Okay."

She kissed his belly, running her tongue in and out and around his navel, then down lower. As he had done to her, she wet his pubic hair thoroughly before finding his now stiffened penis with her tongue. She licked the swollen head, then ran her tongue up and down the smooth underside. Finally, with a loud

"Umm," she took him in her mouth and began to suck him wetly. . . .

In the room next door Dan Fisher was awake. He had moved the room's straight-backed chair over by the window and was sitting there, staring down at the main street. He was thinking about what Canyon O'Grady had said about friendship and loyalty. For the first time since he had been appointed sheriff he was starting to think that maybe he didn't really want the job. Maybe he didn't *deserve* it. He was also starting to feel guilty about the relationship he'd had with Olivia, *and* about loving her.

He wondered if he had time to make up for all of it.

Canyon lay with Mandy's head on his shoulder. His guess was that she planned to spend the night. He didn't mind. It was not something he would want every night, but once in a while he didn't mind having a warm body next to him while he slept. He wondered where her father thought she was, though.

With everything that was going on, that was the last thing he needed, to have an irate father after him with a shotgun.

21

In the morning Canyon made slow love to Mandy, having uppermost in his mind *her* pleasure. He wanted to give her something to remember, in the event he never returned to Watley.

Mandy left first, and then Canyon went down the hall to knock on Fisher's door. When the man answered it was obvious that he had gotten very little sleep. His eyes were red, and there were dark circles under his eyes.

"Are you ready?" Canyon asked.

"Ready as I'll ever be."

As Fisher stepped out into the hall Canyon asked, "Did you get any sleep?"

"No," Fisher said. "Let's go."

Fisher obviously didn't want to talk about what had kept him awake, so Canyon didn't press the issue.

They left the hotel and walked down to the livery stable. Canyon saddled Cormac and Wilmot's horse. Fisher saddled his horse, and then asked the kid who worked at the livery which horse was the sheriff's.

"That one," the kid said, pointing to a big bay mare, "but I don't think—"

"It's all right," Fisher said, showing the kid his badge, "the sheriff asked me to saddle his horse for him. Don't worry about it."

The kid backed off while Fisher saddled Bates's horse. That done they walked the horses out and down to the sheriff's office. When they entered they saw Wilmot sitting behind the sheriff's desk.

"Where's Bates?" Fisher asked.

"He's in the back," Wilmot said. "He's in one piece. Go and check if you want."

Fisher took a step, as if he was going to do just that, then stepped back and said, "No, it's all right. I'll take your word for it."

Wilmot looked at O'Grady, who shrugged his shoulders and shook his head. He didn't know what was going on in Fisher's head, either.

"We've got the horses outside," Canyon said.

"I'll get Bates and we can be on our way," Wilmot said.

Earlier that morning Sam and Carl January rode into Watley while the town was still asleep.

"We need to find someplace we can have a clear view of the jailhouse from," Sam said.

"I know just the place," Carl said.

"Where?"

Carl pointed, and when Sam saw where his brother was pointing he said, "Yeah."

Canyon was going to tell Fisher to keep his eye out for the deputy, but decided not to.

"I'll watch for the deputy," he said instead, and stepped outside.

Fisher stood there and waited until Wilmot returned with Sheriff Bates in tow.

"It's time to pay the piper, Bates," Wilmot said.

"What?"

"Time to do what you said you'd do," Wilmot said.

"Don't worry," Bates said. "I'll do what I said, but then you gotta let me go."

"To do what, Bates?" Wilmot asked. "To go where?"

"Whataya mean where?" Bates asked. "Back here. This is where I live. I'm the sheriff here."

"For what that's worth," Wilmot said. "Come on, let's move."

They walked Bates to the door and outside, where Wilmot asked Canyon, "See anything?"

"No deputy."

"Piece of shit deputy," Bates said. "When I get back he's fired."

"Mount up, Bates," Wilmot said.

All four men stepped down and approached their horses. O'Grady was the first to mount up, followed by Fisher. Because he had only one arm it took Wilmot a little longer to mount up.

Bates had his foot in his stirrup and was swinging his other leg up and over his saddle when they all heard the shot. Bates paused with that second leg in the air, and then fell backward off his horse. He struck the ground with the kind of thud that left no doubt that he was dead.

"Damn it!" Wilmot said, lookng down at the dead man. He still had not mounted up.

"Where did that shot come from?" Fisher demanded, looking around wildly.

More important, Canyon thought, would there be any more?

Being the better shot of the two it was Sam January who took the shot, taking Sheriff Bates right out of his stirrup.

"Good shot, brother Sam," Carl said.

"Thanks, brother Carl. Ya know, I can take the one-armed sheriff from here easy—"

"Let's not press our luck, Sam," Carl said, patting his brother on the back. Carl was the older brother, and when the two were alone it was usually he who made the decisions. "We can get away before they even figured out what happened."

"Yeah, I guess you're right," Sam said, lowering the rifle. "They'll never find us now, anyway."

They got up, hurried to the back of the hotel roof, went down through a hatch, down a flight of steps to the back of the hotel, where they had left their horses.

"Damn it," Wilmot said, again. He was sure Bates was dead, but he leaned over him and checked anyway.

O'Grady shouted at Fisher, "You go north, I'll go south."

They wheeled their horses around and rode in their appointed directions, but Canyon already doubted they would find anything. Whoever had shot Bates—the January brothers, mostly likely—had done the smart thing. They hit their target with the first shot and then lit out.

Most likely the shot had come from a roof, but since they had no idea which roof it was very unlikely they would be able to catch anyone before they got away.

Canyon rode Cormac up and down some alleys and checked behind some buildings. When he got to the hotel he found some fresh tracks there. He could follow these tracks, of course, but there was no way he could be sure that they were made by Bates's killers. He noted a mark in the track left by the hind leg of one of the horses, then turned his horse and rode back to the sheriff's office.

A crowd had gathered by the time he returned, and Fisher was already there.

"Anything?" he asked Fisher.

"No, nothing."

"Me, neither."

"We've got to get moving," Wilmot said to both of them. They were still mounted and he was on the ground.

"To where?" Canyon asked.

"Remember what the girl, Mandy, said yesterday about the farmer?"

"That's right," Canyon said, "the Burke place."

"We've got to get out there and talk to him. He might be able to give us some idea what direction to go in. We might be able to find some fresh tracks from that point."

"Sounds like our only chance," Fisher said.

"Right," Wilmot said.

He retrieved his horse and worked it through the crowd, then mounted up. They left Bates and the crowd behind and rode for the Burke farm.

22

As the three riders were approaching the farmhouse, the front door was opened and a man stepped out. He was holding a shotgun, and he looked ready and willing to use it.

They slowed down and walked their horses up to the house.

"What do you men want?" the man demanded. He looked to be in his forties, a tall, slender man with work-hardened hands and leathery skin. His face bore the scars of a recent pistol-whipping.

"Are you Mr. Burke?" O'Grady asked.

"That's right," the man said, gruffly. "State your business or move on."

"Mr. Burke, we're looking for the same men we understand abducted your wife about three weeks back. We'd like to ask you for your help."

"What do you know about my wife?"

"Only that she was abducted by some men. We believe two of these men were Sam and Carl January. Do those names sound familiar?"

"No."

"Maybe if I describe them to you," Canyon said, and proceeded to do so.

"That's them," Burke said. "Who told you about this?"

"A girl named Mandy Collins."

"I know Mandy."

"Mr. Burke," Canyon said, "we'd like to get your wife back for you."

"She's dead," the man said bitterly.

"Why do you say that?"

"She must be dead by now."

"Maybe not," Canyon said. "She might still be alive, Mr. Burke. If there's a chance that she is, we'd like you to help us."

"I don't know you men . . ."

O'Grady pointed to Fisher and said, "This man is the sheriff of Rayford, Colorado." To support the statement Fisher showed the man his badge. Canyon then pointed to Wilmot and said, "This man lost his arm to injuries these men caused him. As you can see, Mr. Burke, we have our own reasons for wanting to catch these men, just as you yourself have."

Burke hesitated a moment, then lowered his shotgun.

"I couldn't do anything to stop them," he said. "They rode up on us, five of them, with guns. I couldn't do anything. Afterward, I still couldn't do anything. I don't know anything about tracking. I went to the sheriff, but he did nothing."

"We intend to find them, Mr. Burke," Canyon said. "With your help it might be easier."

Burke looked up at Canyon and said, "What do you want me to do?"

"Think back to that day," Wilmot said, leaning forward in his saddle. "I know they pistol-whipped you, but did you see which way they went when they left?"

"I was on the ground," Burke said. "I couldn't seem to move, but I wasn't unconscious. They rode west, over that bluff. I was lying on the ground with my head turned that way, and I watched them ride until they disappeared over it. They went west."

"Let's go west," Wilmot said to O'Grady and Fisher.

"Mr. Burke, the other three men with them: Could you describe them? Tell us what relationship the men had to each other? Such as who appeared to be in charge? Could you tell us all that?"

"I could . . ." Burke said.

After a moment Canyon said, "Would you?"

"I will," Burke said, "on one condition."

"What's that, sir?" Canyon asked.

"That you let me ride with you."

"No offense meant, Mr. Burke," Fisher said, "but you're a farmer, you're not—"

"I can handle a shotgun," Burke said, "and they have my wife. If, as you say, you can find them and my wife is still alive, I have a right to be there."

O'Grady looked at Wilmot and said, "Tom?"

"Seems to me he's got a right," Wilmot said.

O'Grady turned his head and said, "Fisher?"

Fisher hesitated, then said, "Hell, we could use the extra gun."

"Just gimme a minute to mount up," Burke said, stepping down off his porch, "and I'll tell you what you want to know on the way."

When the Januarys got back to their camp they went right to Boudreau's cabin and knocked on the door.

"Come!" they heard him call.

They entered, but Boudreau wasn't in the room.

"Back here," he called from the other room.

Sam and Carl January walked to the doorway and stopped short when they saw what was happening on the bed. Boudreau had the big blonde woman naked and on her hands and knees and was pounding into her from behind. The woman's face was buried in the pillow, but they could still hear her moans and cries. Her big breasts were hanging down and swaying, and her big butt was up in the air. Boudreau was naked and on his knees behind her, and it was obvious that he was buried in her.

"Just . . . give me . . . a . . . minute," Boudreau said.

Helpless to move, the two brothers stood there and watched as Boudreau moved faster and faster, slamming into the woman harder and harder until suddenly the man let out a great groan, and the woman screamed into the pillow.

Neither of the brothers had ever seen anything like it before, and both of their groins were tight.

"Jesus . . ." Sam said, and Carl merely reached and wiped the saliva from his chin.

Boudreau withdrew from the woman and got off the bed, and even semi-erect as it was now, he had a huge cock, purple and heavily veined, and glistening from the woman's juices. It wobbled back and forth as the man walked over to a chair, retrieved his trousers, and pulled them on.

"Outside," Boudreau said, meaning the other room. "Let's give the lady some privacy while she tries to recover from the fucking I just gave her."

Proudly he walked into the next room, picked up a cigar and lighted it. When he had it going the way he liked it he turned to them and said, "So?"

"Uh, sorry we interrupted you, Boudreau," Carl said.

"That's okay," the man said, "I was almost done, anyway. What do you want?"

"We took care of that problem, like you told us," Sam said.

"Are you sure?"

"Dead sure," Carl said, and both brothers laughed.

In the other room Paula Burke curled herself up into a ball on the bed and hoped that Boudreau was finished with her for the day, but she knew that was a vain hope. He hadn't yet made her use her mouth on him, and he'd taken to doing that every day for the past week. Compared to that she almost didn't mind the rest, but he was so big she could hardly fit him in her mouth, and when he came she always choked, unable to take it all in. When that happened he accused her of spitting it out and not liking it, and then she had to try and assure him that she did like it. He had told her that if she wasn't convincing in her claims he was going to "fuck her with the handle of a bull whip," and she believed him.

She just wished she could get her hands on something sharp. She had tried to hide a fork once, and ever since then he made her eat with her hands.

Oh, why didn't God just let her die?

When the Januarys left the cabin Sam said, "Jesus, I need me a woman."

"Me, too."

"We could go to Watley if it wasn't for all the fuss," Sam lamented.

"We could go to Lubbock," Carl suggested.

"That's better'n fifty miles away," Sam said. "By the time we got there I'd be too tired to do anything with a woman."

"I suppose," Carl said.

"I guess we just better go and tell Peters and Dawson what we saw, huh?"

"Yeah," Carl said, "they'll be so jealous they'll bust!"

"God," Sam said as they walked away from the cabin, "that woman sure has got a body . . ."

"Like no whore I ever seen," Carl said.

"You think all them farm women got bodies like that?" his brother asked.

"Must be all the hard work."

"Yeah," Sam agreed, and then he said, "Hey, you suppose there's some other farm near here?"

While they rode over the rise Burke had indicated, the farmer told them about the five men who had pistol-whipped him and taken his wife.

"The two you're talkin' about?" he said. "They seemed to me to be real dumb. I mean, I'm no genius, but they were downright dumb."

If it had indeed been the Januarys who shot Bates that morning, Canyon thought that they had been anything but dumb then, but then in committing murder they might have been in their element and acted instinctively.

"The other two, they just did what they were told and kept quiet."

"So the fifth man was in charge?" O'Grady asked.

"Oh, yeah," Burke said, "he was definitely in charge. He gave the order for the others to beat me down, and then he had them lift Paula up onto the back of his horse."

"Did you hear any names, Mr. Burke?" Fisher asked.

"No, no names. Sorry."

"What did they call the leader?" Wilmot asked.

"Boss," Burke said, "just Boss."

"Can you describe him, Mr. Burke?" Canyon said.

"You fellas got to start callin' me Andy," Burke said. "The leader, he was real tall. Even though he didn't get down from his horse, you could see that. He was also very thin. He took his hat off to mop his brow once, and I could see that he had thick, black hair that came to a point, here."

"A widow's peak," Canyon said.

"Is that what it's called?" Burke asked.

"Yes."

"Well, he had it, then."

"And the others?"

"Well . . ." Burke said, and went on to describe the other four men. His descriptions of the January brothers were perfect. The other two men did not sound like anything special. The Januarys, however, were both huge men, one bigger than the other.

"That's them," Wilmot said.

They came down the other side of the rise and continued to ride west. They rode for an hour before Canyon spotted the tracks on the ground.

"Hold it," he said.

They all stopped and he dismounted. He told them all to stay back so they wouldn't trample the tracks. He went down on one knee to examine the sign. They were fairly fresh, and they seemed to be coming from the direction of Watley. The clincher, however, was when he spotted a familiar mark inside one of the tracks. It was sort of a half moon cut, and it matched perfectly the mark he had seen in the tracks behind the hotel.

"What do we have, Canyon?" Wilmot asked, very anxiously.

He looked up at Wilmot and said, "We've got *them*, Tom."

23

They followed the tracks for two hours until they came to a canyon.

"Think they're in there?" Wilmot asked.

"That'd be my guess," Canyon said.

"Well, let's go in and get them," Andy Burke said.

"Whoa, Andy," Canyon said. "Before we do anything we've got to find out if they have a lookout."

"Jesus, I hope not," Wilmot said, sounding worried.

"Why?" Fisher asked.

"Because if they do, and he knows what he's doin', he must've seen us a mile off, already."

O'Grady knew that Wilmot was right. However, the location of the canyon was so remote that there was a chance that they didn't think they needed a lookout.

"Okay," Canyon said, "I'll go and take a look. The rest of you stay here."

"Why you?" Fisher asked.

"Hey, for once Dan and I agree. Why you?"

"You want me to spell it out?" Canyon asked. "I've got more experience than Fisher, and *two* arms, Tom. There's some climbing involved."

Wilmot compressed his lips and then said, "Well . . . all right."

"Wait here and don't move around," Canyon said, mostly for Burke's benefit. "Mr. Burke, do what these two gentlemen tell you and you'll be fine. Oh, and keep in mind that they don't like each other, but they do work well together."

Burke cast a worried look at Wilmot and Fisher, but said, "I'll remember that."

Canyon took a pair of moccasins out of his saddlebags and put them on. He'd be moving over rock and slate, and moccasins would make no sounds, whereas boots would.

He looked at Wilmot and said, "See you in a little bit."

"Be careful, Canyon."

O'Grady moved cautiously toward the mouth of the canyon, keeping his eyes open for a lookout. There were several vantage points that would have been fine for a lookout, but no matter where he looked he didn't see one. Unless the man was completely hidden from sight, he soon became convinced that there was no lookout posted. All he had to do now was go back and tell the others, but before he did that he decided to take a look down into the canyon itself.

Instead of continuing to the mouth of the canyon he moved for high ground, moving soundlessly on his moccasin-clad feet. When he reached the proper height he moved to the edge on his belly and looked down to the canyon floor.

He saw a cabin and four men camped outside of it. There was a small tent and a buckboard. Off to one side was a corral and inside were seven horses. It figured that the leader of the gang was inside the cabin, possibly with Paula Burke. Five of the horses would be saddle stock, while two were the team that pulled the buckboard. The team probably held stolen merchandise, and/or ammunition and weapons.

A good man with a rifle could pick some of them off at this range. Several good men with rifles could pick all of them off easily. He couldn't rely on Burke from this distance, and Wilmot was a question mark. He didn't know how good Fisher was with a rifle. If he tried to pick off the four men outside the tent, he was bound to miss one. Also, once the shooting started the man inside the tent would have plenty of time to kill the woman.

He pushed himself back from the ledge, then got up and made his way back to the others.

"Jesus, I was just about to come after you," Wilmot said when Canyon reappeared.

"What happened?" Fisher asked.

"Did you see my wife?" Burke asked.

Before answering Canyon took a swig of water from his canteen. It was oppressively hot among the rocks.

"I didn't see a lookout," he said, "which, of course, doesn't mean there isn't one; it just means I didn't see one. However, we'll move on the assumption that there is none."

He went on to tell them what he saw on the canyon floor.

"So you didn't see my wife?" Burke said afterward.

"No, and I didn't see the gang leader—or, at least, the fifth man. He could be inside with her. Two of the men I did see are big enough to be the January boys."

"Well, how do you want to do this?" Wilmot asked. "Pick them off one by one?"

"If we try that there's a possibility that the fifth man will have time to kill Mrs. Burke."

"Assuming that Mrs. Burke is alive," Fisher said.

"Yes," Canyon said, "and we *are* assuming that."

"Then how do we get her out?" Burke asked.

"I thought about that on the way back," Canyon said. "One of us has to get down to the canyon floor and get close to them on foot."

"That will have to be done in the dark," Wilmot said.

"Right," Canyon said. "Once I'm in place—"

"Why you again?" Fisher demanded.

"Because I'm the best qualified, Fisher," Canyon said, impatiently.

"He's right, Dan," Wilmot said. "We'd break a leg trying to get around those rocks in the dark."

"But—"

"Just listen!" Wilmot said. "Go ahead, Canyon."

"Once I'm in position," O'Grady said, "we'll have to wait for daylight. You'll have to assume that I got inside the house, and start shooting."

"What if we don't get them all with our initial volley?" Wilmot asked.

"Then we'll likely be in for a siege," Canyon said, "but I hope by then to have control of the cabin."

"So we're not gonna do anything until tomorrow morning?"

"I can't move until it's dark, Mr. Burke," Canyon said, "and that's correct, you can't do anything until morning."

"And what if they start to move before then?" Fisher asked.

Canyon looked at him and said, "Then all bets are off and we'll just have to do the best we can." He looked at them all and said, "We'd better withdraw a bit, and take turns keeping watch while the others rest. It's going to be a long night."

At dusk O'Grady started moving for the canyon mouth. He left his rifle behind for Burke and took the farmer's shotgun with him. He didn't know how well Burke would do with the rifle, but he could certainly use the shotgun effectively at close range. He also took a knife with him. Still wearing the moccasins, he made his way to the canyon mouth and waited there for total darkness to fall.

Once it was dark, with just a sliver of a moon in the sky, he moved cautiously into the canyon mouth. From where he was he could see that they had made two separate campfires, which were throwing off a good amount of light. The house, however, was beyond the reach of the light, although there was light coming from inside.

The house was between him and the campfires, and the horses were beyond the fire. That left little chance that the horses would notice him and give him away.

He continued moving forward, cautiously, soundlessly, until voices started coming to him from the campfires. He couldn't make out what they were saying, but as he got closer to the house the drone of voices got louder.

He couldn't see any movement from the house, or hear any sounds—that is, until he got much closer. He heard a man, then, moaning and talking. He also heard a woman's voice. She wasn't talking, she was simply making . . . sounds. As he got closer still, the sounds the man and woman were making left little doubt as to what was going on.

He was able to move in total darkness until he was hidden from view by the cabin, so that even if the men looked his way they wouldn't see him now. He finally reached the cabin and pressed his back to the wall. He moved along the wall until he reached a window, and when he looked inside his blood went cold.

A man was standing naked in the center of the

room, and crouched before him, also naked, was a big, blonde woman. The man's back was to the window, blocking Canyon's view of the woman, but the red-haired agent could imagine what the woman was doing. The man was moaning, holding her head with both hands. He originally thought that the woman was moaning, as well, but soon determined that she was crying instead. It was evident that she was being forced against her will to perform this act on the man, and she was doing so with some difficulty.

Every fiber of his being wanted to burst into that cabin through the window and fire both barrels at the man. He would have done so even as the man was still in her mouth, because he knew she'd get some satisfaction from *feeling* the man die that way. However, soon after that they'd probably both be dead, as the other four men rushed into the cabin, and in the darkness the other men—Wilmot, Fisher, and Burke—would be powerless to offer any assistance.

Canyon moved away from the window, pressed his back to the wall, held the shotgun tightly in both hands, closed his eyes tightly, and tried to drown out the sounds the woman was making.

24

Canyon spent the night crouched down, his back against the wall of the cabin, and he never once had to move to avoid being discovered. The four men camped outside the cabin never once entered the cabin, or came near it, probably by standing order of their leader. Once, during the night, Canyon again heard Paula Burke moaning and crying out, and heard the man making sounds like a rutting bull. He did not bother to move to the window to look because he did not want to see what was going on. He only hoped that they would be able to rescue Paula Burke, and that she would be able to go back to living a normal life with her husband in spite of the ordeal she had been put through.

At dawn Wilmot, who had taken the last watch, woke Fisher and Burke and said, "It's time."

Together, the three men started moving toward high ground. Halfway there Wilmot stopped their progress.

"What is it?" Fisher asked.

"You still a good shot, Dan?"

"Sure," Fisher said, "why?"

"One of us should be down on the canyon floor with him, ready to help."

"And you figure it should be you?"

"That's right."

"Why?"

"Because you're a better shot with two hands than I am with one, Dan."

"What about me?" Burke asked. "You're probably a better shot with one hand than I am with two."

"I'm also better qualified to go down to the canyon floor than you are, Andy."

"I don't know if I'll be able to hit anything from up there," Burke said frankly.

"That's all right, Andy," Wilmot said. "Just keep firing as fast as you can, and make a lot of noise. All right?"

"Sure," the farmer said, dejectedly.

Wilmot put his hand on the man's shoulder and said, "We'll get her back." He knew how he would have felt if it was Olivia in that cabin, so he said it again. "We'll get her back—I promise."

Canyon moved to the front of the cabin and peered around the corner. From what he could see the other four men were still asleep. He moved back to the window and looked inside. The woman was alone on the bed. The man, the leader, was nowhere to be seen.

He moved to another window now, so he could see into the front room, and saw the man sleeping against the wall on a pallet. Apparently he kept the woman in the other room for his pleasure, but didn't sleep with her. That suited him just fine.

He went back to the window to the back room and tried it. As he had hoped it was unlocked. They obviously felt there was no reason to lock it, and that Paula could get nowhere, naked and on foot. He slid it open as quietly as he could and climbed into the room. The thing he had to do now was wake Paula without having her give him away.

He approached the bed, keeping the shotgun in one hand, and when he reached her he quickly put his hand over her mouth. He expected her to react in surprise, but she simply opened her eyes and looked up at him. Her eyes looked dead. She was probably so used to being awakened for sex that nothing surprised her anymore.

"Paula?" Canyon said.

She didn't answer, just continued to stare at him.

"Are you Paula Burke?" he asked.

He thought she wasn't going to answer again, and then she simply nodded her head.

"I'm here with your husband, Mrs. Burke," he said. "We're going to get you out. Do you understand?"

She nodded again.

"If you cry out when I remove my hand, I'll be killed. Understand?"

She nodded again, and he removed his hand. He then realized that he was sitting on the bed with this big, naked woman, pressing up against her. Even in this situation it was disconcerting. She smelled sharply of sex and sweat, but that didn't matter. He still felt his body reacting.

"Where is my husband?" she asked.

"He's nearby," Canyon said. "Listen to me carefully, because very soon we're going to have to move."

Tom Wilmot made his way to the mouth of the canyon but did not enter. At the first sound of gunshots he would move into the mouth and start running for the camp as fast as he could.

He settled in to wait.

Fisher and Burke worked their way up to a point where they had a clear view of the camp and the cabin below. When Burke asked, "When do we shoot?" Fisher realized that the entire plan now hinged on him. He had to decide when the time was right to fire, setting the whole thing in motion.

The four men on the canyon floor were still wrapped in their bedrolls, and Fisher could not bring himself to fire on them in that helpless position, no matter who they were or what they had done.

"We'll wait until they begin to stir," Fisher said. "Until they get up."

"Why don't we wake them up?" Burke asked. "They'd sure be shocked and confused."

Of course, Fisher thought. They didn't have to fire *at* the men, they simply had to fire, waking them up. Burke was right, they wouldn't know what hit them, and they'd be disoriented. Easy targets.

"That's a good idea," Fisher said. "Let's wake them up." He shouldered his rifle and in a sudden flash of inspiration he said, "Aim for the tent."

The first volley of shots struck the tent, penetrated the fabric, and struck the crates that were inside.

"What the hell—" Sam January said, coming awake.

Around him his brother and the other two men also awoke confused, looking around to see what was happening.

"We're being shot at!" Peters shouted.

"From where?" Dawson demanded.

They threw off their blankets and stood up, guns in hand.

"Up there!" Carl January cried out.

They all raised their guns to return fire when suddenly a bullet hit Peters in the shoulder, spinning him around. As he fell he found himself facing the tent, which was still being chewed up by bullets.

"Oh, Jesus," he said, as he realized what was inside the tent, and how close they were to it.

"Run!" he shouted, but he was too late. A stray bullet finally struck a crate containing the dynamite, and the tent blew.

At the sound of the first volley Wilmot broke into the canyon and started running toward the camp. He was halfway there when the tent suddenly exploded. The air filled with smoke, fire, and debris, and as he continued to run forward the debris began to fall around him. There was a secondary explosion, as another crate went, and now he couldn't see the men who were in the camp.

But he kept running.

"Let's go," Canyon said to Paula as the first shots sounded. He had removed his shirt and given it to her. She was so tall, though, that it barely covered her round hips and thighs.

He pushed her to the window so she could climb out. As he was helping her the door from the other room slammed open and Boudreau stepped into the room, gun in hand.

"No," she said, seeing Boudreau over her shoulder.

Canyon had one hand on her arm, helping her out the window, but he turned quickly and fired the shotgun one-handed.

Outside Wilmot was working his way through the smoke. There were shots coming from the ridge above, and from inside the camp, but no one really had any idea what they were shooting at. Wilmot continued his forward motion, staying low and hoping that a stray shot wouldn't kill him by accident.

Suddenly he was face-to-face with one of the January brothers.

"You!" Sam January said in surprise.

Wilmot lifted his gun and fired. His bullet struck January in the chest and he fired again, putting one in the man's stomach.

"Die!" he said as the man fell.

He kept moving forward, into the smoke, which was shifting, but not thinning. The remains of the tent were in flames, giving off great gobs of smoke, and a burning piece of debris had landed on the roof of the shack, which was now in flames as well.

Wilmot saw a great hulking mass appear in front of him and he fired again. Carl January cried out as the bullet found its mark. The one-armed man was about to fire again when he tripped over something and went sprawling. He looked at what he had fallen over and saw a man. The man was bleeding from a shoulder wound, but what had killed him was a piece of wood from an exploded crate. It had entered his stomach like an arrow and killed him.

Wilmot looked around him frantically. He knew that two of them were dead, and he had injured the other January. There was still a fourth man around somewhere.

The shotgun blast hit Boudreau squarely in the chest and threw him back into the other room.

"Come on," Canyon said to Paula, "out."

"No," she said, bringing her other leg back into the cabin. "I want to see him."

"Paula—"

"I want to see him dead!" she screamed, and he

saw that there was no arguing with her. Anyway, she probably did deserve to see the man dead.

"All right."

They entered the other room and she walked over to Boudreau's body. The man looked as if his chest had exploded, and he was quite dead, but that didn't stop her from kicking him in the head again and again until she had no strength to continue.

At that point Canyon realized that the cabin was on fire.

He moved to Paula and put his arms around her. "We have to get out," he said, and half carried her to the door.

As he opened the door and stepped out he saw all the smoke outside. He discarded the shotgun, drew his gun with one hand, and took her hand in his other. "Stay behind me," he said.

He moved through the smoke and the first thing he saw was Wilmot sitting on the ground, a dead man at his feet. Behind his friend was one of the Januarys. The man was bleeding from a bullet wound in his side, but he was still getting ready to blow Wilmot's head off from behind.

"Tom!" Canyon shouted, and he fired at Carl January.

Wilmot turned in time to see O'Grady's shot strike January right in the face. By the time the ex-lawman scrambled to his feet, January had hit the ground.

Wilmot looked at O'Grady and said, "I think there's one more."

"Be careful."

"Get her out of here!" Wilmot shouted and disappeared into the smoke.

By this time the entire cabin was in flames, giving off black plumes of smoke. Canyon couldn't go after

Wilmot, not with Paula Burke in tow, so he pulled her along and headed for the mouth of the canyon.

When they got far enough away from the camp the smoke was thin and he could see that they were headed in the right direction.

Suddenly, Paula Burke stopped.

"What's wrong?"

"I can't see my husband," she said.

"He'll be here soon—"

"No," she said, still resisting, "you don't understand. I can't let him see me."

"Paula—"

"You don't know the things that animal did to me!" she said.

He didn't want to tell her that he did know. That would only humiliate her further.

"Paula, I can imagine what happened—or maybe I can't, but I can tell you one thing. Your husband loves you. He'll take you back no matter what."

She stared at him for a moment, then cast her eyes downward.

"It will be up to you how much you tell him," Canyon said, "but anything's better than what you've been through. Now, come on."

She looked at him and nodded. They walked to the mouth of the canyon together, where Dan Fisher and Andy Burke were waiting. Burke rushed forward and grabbed his wife and they slid to the ground, hugging each other tightly.

"Where's Tom?" Fisher asked.

"He's still in there, finishing up," Canyon said.

"Should we go in and help him?"

"I don't think so."

Fisher looked at O'Grady and said, "You'll be glad to know that when we get back to Rayford I'm going to give up the sheriff's job, and recommend they give it back to Tom."

"That's good," Canyon said.

"Then I'm going to volunteer to be his deputy again."

"That's even better."

Maybe having his job back would help Tom deal with whatever was going to happen between him and Olivia. As for Canyon he was satisfied that he had done all he could for his friend. He decided never to tell Tom about what happened with Olivia, and he didn't think Olivia would either. She wanted to leave Tom, but she never said anything about hating him. Canyon doubted she would ever deliberately hurt him—and who knew? Maybe when Tom got back he and Olivia would talk things over and Olivia would change her mind. He still felt that they were both his friends and wished only the best for them.

He also decided that he would head directly to Washington from here, and not go back to Rayford with Tom and Fisher. Olivia was still his friend, but he wasn't up to seeing her again, just yet.

O'Grady and Fisher looked back at the camp, which was still enveloped by smoke, and just when Canyon was thinking that maybe they should go and help Wilmot, the man appeared from out of the smoke like an apparition.

He approached them, his gun in his hand but held down by his side. His face was streaked with black, and he appeared uninjured.

When he reached them he smiled at Canyon and holstered his gun.

"It's done," he said.

"Good, Tom," Canyon said. "Let's go home."

(0451)

CANYON O'GRADY RIDES ON

☐ **CANYON O'GRADY #9: COUNTERFEIT MADAM by Jon Sharpe** (167252—$3.50)

☐ **CANYON O'GRADY #10: GREAT LAND SWINDLE by Jon Sharpe** (168011—$3.50)

☐ **CANYON O'GRADY #11: SOLDIER'S SONG by Jon Sharpe** (168798—$3.50)

☐ **CANYON O'GRADY #12: RAILROAD RENEGADES by Jon Sharpe** (169212—$3.50)

☐ **CANYON O'GRADY #13: ASSASSIN'S TRAIL by Jon Sharpe** (169646—$3.50)

☐ **CANYON O'GRADY #15: DEATH RANCH by Jon Sharpe** (170490—$3.50)

☐ **CANYON O'GRADY #16: BLOOD AND GOLD by Jon Sharpe** (170946—$3.50)

☐ **CANYON O'GRADY #17: THE KILLERS' CLUB by Jon Sharpe** (171314—$3.50)

☐ **CANYON O'GRADY #18: BLOOD BOUNTY by Jon Sharpe** (171985—$3.50)

☐ **CANYON O'GRADY #19: RIO GRANDE RANSOM by Jon Sharpe** (172396—$3.50)

☐ **CANYON O'GRADY #20: CALIFORNIA VENGEANCE by Jon Sharpe** (173058—$3.50)